Murdered Innocence
The Maryann Mitchell Murder Revisited

ISBN 978-1-300-34652-4

ACKNOWLEDGMENTS

My husband and daughters

George Beetham, editor <u>The Review</u>

Lt. Michael Gilbert, Montgomery County Detectives, Forensic Unit, Montgomery County,PA

Donna Cassatt, Kelly Lawver, Patricia O'Tanger, Office of the Deputy Court Administrator, Adams County, PA

The Philadelphia Innocence Project

This book is dedicated to
The memory of
Maryann Mitchell

And my father,
Philadelphia Police Officer
John Patrick Tinneny

PROLOGUE

This work is a theory regarding the 1959 murder of 16-year-old Maryann Mitchell who lived in the Manayunk section of Philadelphia. It is based on actual events; some names have been changed unless they were a matter of public record. On September 1, 1960 Elmo Lee Smith, was sentenced to death by electrocution for Maryann's brutal murder. On the evening of April 2, 1962 the sentence was carried out. The 41 year old convicted murderer was put to death in Bellefonte, Pennsylvania at the Rockview Penitentiary, strapped to a solid oak electric chair. Elmo Smith would be the last of 350 men and women in the State of Pennsylvania who had been executed in the electric chair since 1915.

My father believed, until his dying day in 1988, that Elmo Lee Smith did not murder Maryann Mitchell. For most of my life I thought he was alone in that belief until I began researching the homicide and found that there were many who, like my father, believed that Elmo Smith was innocent.

In September 2010, at the request of Al Jarvis, Maryann's cousin, who lives in Arizona, I attempted to secure the case file of Maryann's murder through the Office of the District Attorney in Montgomery County, Pennsylvania under The Right to Know Law of 2008. The request was denied. I appealed. The appeal was denied citing that The RTKL, exempts from release "(a) record of an agency relating to or resulting in a criminal investigation".

Much of the information contained in this book was gleaned from newspaper accounts published in The

Review, the hometown newspaper of Manayunk and The Gettysburg Gazette that carried daily coverage of the trial which was held in Adams County, Pennsylvania. Most importantly research was done in Gettysburg, using the original trial transcripts. As is the fact in looking back at any event, it is very difficult to discern fact from fiction, reality from rumor. In the case of the Maryann Mitchell homicide and the conviction of Elmo Smith, as her murderer, there was a great deal of media coverage, and even Court testimony that evolved in differing versions as events unfolded. It is not my intention in this book to convince anyone of Elmo Smith's innocence. It *is* my intention to present the events as they were reported in the media and in trial testimony, in light of my father's theory.

Chapter 1: Manayunk in '59

"Ah she seemed like a sweet girl, always laughing, her and her friends", said Frank Talbot. *"Ya know Jack, I get to know all the kids around here, Friday night's the big night at the Roxy for them. It's a shame what happened to her"*. My father, Philadelphia Police Officer Jack Tinneny was on the "A" bus which had just recently been converted from a trackless trolley bus route here in Manayunk and Roxborough and Frank was the driver. The Tinneny and Talbot families were neighbors and members of Holy Family Parish in Manayunk. That was fifty-three years ago and I still remember pieces of those days. Most certainly I remember conversations with my father throughout his life and his ultimate frustration that the killer of Maryann Mitchell had gotten away with murder, had committed the perfect crime. The most profound part of my father's frustration lay in the fact that the perfection had nothing do with any brilliance on the part of the murderer, but rather, on a string of events and an array of personalities, that, in the end, led to Elmo Smith being made to fit the crime.

Manayunk is a little community nestled in the northwest corner of Philadelphia between Center City and Montgomery County. The row homes there were built on ascending hills steeping upward from the Schuylkill River to Ridge Avenue. Back in the day, it seemed as if there was a Church on every block. And everyone knew everybody. Parents were parents to all of us kids. They watched over us and would correct us if they saw us doing anything wrong. We never called adults by their first names. It was either: Miss, Misses or Mister. If they were close friends of our family we called them Aunt or Uncle.

Many of us were taught by nuns in local parish schools. We attended Mass on Sundays, usually at 9 a.m. That was the children's Mass. Each nationality in our community had its own church and school: Irish, Holy Family and Saint John the Baptist; Italian, Saint Lucy; Polish, Saint Josaphat and German, Saint Mary of the Assumption. If you went to Catholic School you were identified by your parish.

We called the kids that went to Public Schools the "Publics" and we all played together at our playgrounds on the weekends. Hillside was our playground. During the summer days it seemed like we lived at those playgrounds. We kids, the "Publics" and the "Catholics", were like siblings in one big family called "Yunkers". We played softball, baseball, volleyball and basketball. We skate boarded, roller skated and rode our bikes. The big kids played pinochle and chess for hours at Hillside on cement, initial-chiseled game tables complete with cement cylinders for seating.

Back in '59, during the fall and spring, we did homework after school, watched Sally Starr on black and white T.V. sets and always had dinner at five-thirty. At night we watched shows like "I Love Lucy", "Gunsmoke", "Perry Mason", and "Walt Disney Presents". We played marbles, checkers and pick-up sticks, colored in coloring books, with crayons that were kept in old cookie tins and built elaborate houses from mismatched decks of playing cards. We had our Barbie dolls and plastic green soldiers. We took our baths, combed our hair, brushed our teeth, said our prayers and were in bed by nine.

On weekends we would walk up the Ridge to the Roxy for the matinee. On weekend nights the big kids would go to the Roxy for a movie or to a dance at Holy Family or St. John's where vinyl 45s were spun on a record player.

On summer nights we younger kids played street games: Hide-the-belt, jump rope, tug-of-war and hopscotch, while our Moms sat on door stoops and talked. There were plenty of neighborhood kids in each family back then. I was the youngest of seven. Our next door neighbors on either side, the Petrucci family and the Distel family each had four children. It was fun growing up in those streets of Manayunk. At dusk, just when the street lights went on, the big kids walked down to the corner ice cream parlor and brought back .25¢ double-decker ice cream cones for us little kids. At the end of summer the big kids had a ritual of throwing their "Chuks" over the telephone wires.

Winters in the hills of Manayunk were treacherous for adults. But for us kids the hills made for some of the best sledding in Philly. If you were lucky, one of your dads had a car big enough to take a few of you sledding down the golf course at Walnut Lane. That was like Switzerland in Roxborough. We built snowmen in our backyards and dug snow tunnels in the mounds of snow plowed high on our street corners. And then there was Christmas. There was no better time to enjoy family and friends than during Christmas break. No school, no responsibilities, just fun days and nights. We delighted in a winter walk up the Ridge to visit Santa's North Pole Workshop, a 6' x 6' shed to adults, but to us kids it was where we encountered the grand old Mr. Claus each year to ask him for the toys we longed for in our hearts. Each year the visit was captured by a photo with Santa which our parents preserved faithfully in the family photo album. Life was innocent then.

But the joy of Christmas 1959 was cut short by a tragedy, the likes of which the neighborhood of Manayunk, and the families there, had never experienced. On December 28, 1959 16-year-old Maryann Mitchell of DuPont Street in Manayunk was reported missing by her mother shortly after midnight. Two days later her savagely defiled body was found dead in a remote lane in Lafayette Hill, Montgomery County. The violence of her death permeated the city of Philadelphia and the Township of Montgomery County with paralyzing fear. I remember my parents grieving: My mother taking off her glasses to wipe tears from her eyes as she attempted to read the newspaper accounts of the crime. Our town grieved as if each mother and father had lost one of their own children. Our parents hugged us a great deal more in the days following Maryann's murder.

Seven days after her murder, an accused convict on parole, Elmo Lee Smith, was apprehended in connection with the gruesome crime. As fate would have it, my parents knew something of Elmo Lee Smith. Back in 1941 as a young married couple, with a newborn son, my parents rented a third floor apartment at 312 Burnside Street in Manayunk. Elmo Smith, a truck driver, rented the first floor apartment in the same building. My mother recalled how she and Smith argued, almost daily, over his wanting her to not leave the baby stroller inside the first floor vestibule of the building. My mother refused to lug it up to the third floor apartment. None-the-less she could not envision Smith as a brutal murder.

Chapter 2: Into the Night

Monday December 28, 1959

Sophie Sutch walked from her home at 152 DuPont Street to the home of her friend and neighbor Maryann Mitchell at 195 DuPont Street. The night before the girls had gone to a Christmas dance at St. John the Baptist hall. Maryann, 16, was a junior at Cecilian Academy in Mount Airy, a private, Catholic, girls high school. She had just received her class ring. That day she wore a green wool pleated skirt, a wide black leather belt, a gold blouse and a green corduroy jacket. Around her head she wore a flowered scarf and on her feet she wore gray leather Peter Gunn Shoes. Maryann's parents had asked their only child to deliver Christmas gifts to her Aunt Elizabeth Gillespie's home on Houghton Street. Maryann carried a large brown leather handbag that evening. The handbag was a Christmas gift from her classmate Mary Anne Carney. On this day the handbag was like a Santa sack, transporting gifts. Maryann and Sophie left the Mitchell's home on the first leg of their journey which was to the Gillespie home.

The two girls spent a short time there. Upon leaving Maryann's handbag was re-filled with gifts from her Aunt to deliver to her parents. There was an envelope and card for Maryann (which she opened) containing $3.00, there were 4 packs of cigarettes for Edwin Mitchell, and a green scarf with blue ceramic earrings for Sarah Mitchell. Later they would walk to the home of their friend Connie Kerns. Together, the three friends would meet up with Mary Ann Carney at the Roxy Theater on Ridge Avenue to see the movie "South Pacific".

Following the movie the girls walked south on Ridge Avenue (9 blocks), turned left on Rector Street (2 blocks) and made a right on Henry Avenue (2 blocks) to Koller's Kitchen, a small diner at 5826 Henry Avenue which is now Chubby's Steaks. Sophie did not go with them, choosing instead to walk home with a neighborhood boy. It was a rainy night and the girls were soaked. Because of the weather things were slow at the diner. Joseph Salvato was the night manager that evening. Rose Pulkowski was the waitress who served the girls. "*We all did a lot of kidding and had a good time,*" Salvato said. The three girls ordered hamburgers, coffees and malted milks.

Close to 10:20 the girls said goodbye to Salvato and Pulkowski. The three friends left the diner. Connie and Mary Ann walked toward Jamestown Street. Maryann crossed Henry Avenue, walking toward the bus stop which was almost directly across the street from Koller's, a distance of 112 steps. Maryann was believed to have stepped onto an "A" bus. The "A" would take her to Ridge and Leverington Avenues. There she would get the "Z" bus to Manayunk, getting off at Leverington Avenue and Silverwood Street, a block from her home. It was a trip of about 10 minutes.

Maryann's mother, Sara Mitchell, was working that evening at Kenny's Box Company located at Main and Cotton Streets in Manayunk. She had made the decision to work so she and her husband could afford the tuition to send their daughter to Cecilian Academy. Edwin Mitchell, alone and waiting for his daughter, grew uneasy when Maryann had not returned home shortly after the 10:30 pm curfew. By midnight Sarah Mitchell returned home from work and she frantically phoned police to report her daughter missing.

On Tuesday morning, December 29, 1959 the sun rose on one of the darkest days in Manayunk history. Philadelphia Police from the Fifth District had been searching the neighborhood throughout the earliest hours of the morning for the missing 16-year-old described as having auburn hair and hazel eyes, being five feet, four inches tall and weighing approximately one-hundred and ten pounds.

She had never been on a date and had recently questioned her mother, *"Why would boys be interested in me?"* By all accounts Maryann was a rather quiet girl with a close circle of friends. She had attended Saint Josaphat, Catholic Elementary School, prior to attending Cecilian Academy. She was a girl scout in Troop 341 sponsored by the Roxborough Baptist Church. In January of 1958 Maryann was one of thirty girls on a camp-out at Camp Laughing Waters. Mrs. Kathryn Johnson, who was on the Troop Committee for the camping trip as a chaperone, recalled how Maryann, *"though shy and retiring most of the time knew how to enjoy life"*. Mrs. Johnson recalled an event of that trip, *"In the middle of the night three other girls and Maryann decided to carry me and my cot out of the cabin into a field. When I woke up there, I was all alone. The next day Maryann and the girls told how much fun they had in carrying out their sleeping chaperone."* Maryann was especially interested in hospital aid work. She and some other of the girls from her scout troop were scheduled to go to Memorial Hospital on January 9, 1960 to get their instructions as volunteer Candy Stripers, young girls who volunteered to assist patients at the hospital.

The residents of Manayunk had good reason to fear for Maryann. Just eleven days prior, on December 18, 1959 17-year-old Joyce Ann Davis had attended a Christmas party at First Methodist Church on Green Lane. Walking home, she was attacked less than a block from her home at 416 Kingsley Street. The time of the assault was 10:30 pm. She suffered five stab wounds to her right arm. Joyce described her attacker as *"a male, approximately seventeen years of age who drove off in a light color sedan".* Joyce was released from Memorial Hospital on December 23, 1959. Her assailant had not been caught. The attack on Joyce Davis was within four blocks of the bus stop across from Koller's Kitchen, the last location at which Maryann had been seen.

Chapter 3: A Spot of Green

Wednesday December 30, 1959

At approximately 2:30 pm, John Breidenbach, Pat Carlino, Edward Schwartz and Daniel McGuigan, members of a Whitemarsh township highway department work crew, saw a spot of green in a muddy gully five feet off the right of Harts Lane (headlining toward Miquon) and approximately seventy-five feet above Barren Hill Road. In those days Harts Lane at Barren Hill Road ran through a desolate, wooded area without street lighting. It was an area of Lafayette Hill well known to police, in what was otherwise thought to be an idyllic hamlet, bordering the west of Philadelphia. That area of Lafayette Hill was a place where those who did unspeakable acts could walk unnoticed in the cold shadows of nature, protected by the darkness of night.

Frank Rippert of Roxborough, a member of a local archery club with a range on Manor Road, was going through the course on Tuesday morning, March 31, 1959 and missed a target. In searching for his arrow he came upon a department store shopping bag that appeared to have contents in it. Upon opening the bag he found the body of a full term infant wrapped in newspaper and brown paper. The infant had been born alive, wrapped in the paper and left to die. The cause of death was listed as neglect.

On June 19, 1959 two sailors, one from West Conshohocken and the other from Conshohocken, who were home on leave, were committed to Montgomery County Prison in Norristown, PA and held without bail. The two men are accused of abducting a 17-year-old Roxborough girl on Wednesday, June 17, 1959. The girl was walking near her home when the men, riding in a white Chevrolet sedan, offered her a ride home. Instead they drove the girl to Manor Road and assaulted her. Manor Road immediately precedes and runs parallel to Barren Hill Road. The two sailors insisted that the young woman had gone with them voluntarily. All was not as idyllic in the Montgomery County suburb as it seemed.

On this day, Daniel McGuigan walked into the gully for a closer look. The spot of green was rain-soaked clothing on the body of a young woman. Her head and face were covered in blood. Her arms and legs were posed in an outstretched position. On her fingers there were an amethyst ring and a high school ring. She was wearing nylon stockings attached to a portion of a garter belt, her feet were shoeless. Her underpants were draped over her right arm. Her green jumper was pulled up over her chest exposing her naked lower body. On her abdomen, written in what appeared to be red lipstick were the letters "TB" and "101". An arch was drawn above her pubic area with lines radiating from it. Although I have not been able to document through any newspaper articles describing the crime scene, my father stated that there was a Coke soda bottle inside the girl's vagina and a portion of a tree branch protruded out of her rectum.

Whitemarsh Township Chief of Police Edgar Mitchell and Sergeant Lloyd Frankenfield were the first of a group of investigators at the scene. Aware that a 16-year-old Philadelphia girl was missing, officials from Whitemarsh Township notified Philadelphia authorities, alerting them of the discovery of the body. Within the hour, the crime scene would build to a massive assemblage of investigators and reporters from both Montgomery County and Philadelphia. Upon evaluation of the immediate area where the body was found, investigators believed, because of a lack of blood, that the girl was killed at another location and her body was dumped in the gully.

Since the victim was found in Whitemarsh Township, Montgomery County her body was transported to a funeral home within Montgomery County. George Snear of Ardell Funeral Home was called to the location to remove the body to that funeral home which was located at 300 Fayette Street in Conshohocken.

In a 2011 phone interview with Mr. Snear he recalled that, although the details of that day had blurred over time, he did remember clearly that he, *"had never, and would never again, experience chaos as he had experienced it that evening"*. There was a viewing at the funeral home at the same time the body of the young girl was brought into a room there. Shortly after the arrival of the body a Philadelphia Police contingent headed by Chief Inspector John Kelly arrived. With Kelly were George Kronbar, commander of the Homicide Squad, Lieutenant Andrew Walters also of the Homicide Squad and Detectives Edward Rock and Howard Factor of the Philadelphia Northwest Detectives Division. Thomas Moody, Chief of Montgomery County detectives was there heading the investigation. Believing the body to be that of Maryann Mitchell, Detectives Edward Rock and Howard Factor took the two rings and articles of the girl's clothing to the Mitchell home. They were identified by Edwin Mitchell as belonging to Maryann. The high school ring was engraved with the initials "MTM". Mr. Mitchell was then accompanied to the funeral home by the detectives to identify his daughter's body.

Meanwhile, Whitemarsh Police continued investigating the scene, searching the area and surrounding buildings for leads from Ridge Pike to River Road. Specifically, police sought to locate the girl's shoes and parts of a missing garter-belt. All cars that passed the scene were stopped by two police officers; each driver's name was taken and logged.

Later that evening, Montgomery County coroner, Dr. John C. Simpson performed an autopsy on Maryann at the funeral home. He stated that, *"The girl died of a fractured skull and severe slashing of the brain. She also had been "ruptured in two places",* a possible reference to the Coke bottle and the tree branch. *"Her knees were bruised and there was a bruise on her right wrist, as if a car door had been closed on it".* Dr. Simpson estimated that *"she had been dead about 12 hours when found."* That would estimate the time of death as approximately 2:30 am Wednesday, December 30, 1959. Simpson would later testify that, *"the girl died almost instantly from the fatal blow to her head. She could not have lived longer than an hour"*. Upon completion of the autopsy, the body of Maryann was transported to the Modzianowski-J.J. Young Funeral Home located at 118 Grape Street.

Flashlight wielding police continued to search the area surrounding Barren Hill Road and Harts Lane late into the evening, for items that were obviously missing from the victim, specifically her shoes and a portion of the garter belt. At the corner of Ridge Pike and Barren Hill Road, on the grounds of Eagle Lodge Country Club [The Ace Center] Maryann's Peter Gunn shoes and wallet were found.

New Years Eve

Thursday December 31, 1959

Preliminary findings of the autopsy are published in local daily newspapers and nationwide in an Associated Press release. As well, it is reported that, *"police are investigating the possibility that the killer may have been the same man who stabbed 17-year-old stenographer, Joyce Davis, in the same area on December 18."*

This same day, a flat black ballet slipper is found lying on Ridge Avenue approximately 100 feet east of Domino Lane by a young girl and was turned-over to Philadelphia detectives. The shoe is identified by Constance Kerns as hers. Constance said that on the evening prior to Maryann's disappearance the two had attended the dance at St. John the Baptist. The two girls had brought the slippers to dance in. Maryann had placed Constance's slippers into her handbag, intending to return them later. Constance was certain the slippers were in Maryann's handbag the night she disappeared. The finding of the slipper led police to believe that Maryann may have been killed in Roxborough. It is important to note that, the shoe would have lain in this very public, high pedestrian and automobile traffic area, for the three days since Mary Ann was last seen. As well, if the killer had tossed the slipper from the car in which Maryann was abducted, the driver would have detoured off of Henry Avenue, a remote roadway where he could drive unnoticed, onto Ridge Avenue a main thoroughfare populated with both residences and businesses.

Chapter 4: Captain Clarence J. Ferguson

Friday: January 1, 1960

Clarence Ferguson was a friend of the Mitchell family. But this resident of Roxborough was no ordinary neighbor; Clarence J. Ferguson was the head of the Special Investigation Unit of the Philadelphia Police Department or more accurately, "Clarence Ferguson's Special Investigations Squad". A group of empowered, untouchable, unquestionable, detectives who were young and cocky, notoriously referred to as "Fergie's Boys". Ferguson himself was a larger-than-life character who was identifiable by his trademark porkpie hat. A veteran of World War I and at the time of the murder, having served the City of Philadelphia continuously for 41 years, Clarence Ferguson could rightfully boast of having the longest length of service of any man in the Philadelphia Police Department. He himself was empowered, untouchable and unquestionable. He held a total of 81 departmental commendations for outstanding police work at the time of Maryann's murder and was the recipient the "Gangbuster Award" in 1955 for being *the outstanding detective in the nation.*

On November 30, 1959, at Palumbo's restaurant in Philadelphia, Ferguson had been proclaimed by Judge Adrian Bonnelly, president judge of Philadelphia Municipal Court, the largest Municipal Court in Pennsylvania, as the *"biggest man in police work in the whole United States of America."*

That image, though deserved in many respects, was crafted by Ferguson's media mastery. If Ferguson didn't take reporters along on a raid or an important arrest, he was sure to call the newspaper before deadline with details. Back in February of 1956, Ferguson led a raid at the hotel room of Billie Holiday and her husband Louis McKay on charges of being narcotics users and in possession of narcotics, while the famed singer was performing in Philadelphia. Clarence Ferguson himself contacted newspaper reporters informing them of the raid. A photo of the famed singer appeared in Philadelphia newspapers showing Ferguson escorting Holiday following the raid.

A personal friend of entertainer Jimmy "The Snoz" Durante, Ferguson would arrange for Durante to perform a show at Ferguson's parish hall at Immaculate Heart of Mary Church in Andorra. And for Christmas 1959 Durante had given Mrs. Ferguson, Captain Ferguson's wife, a mink stole. In the 1960 editions of The Review, there are 24 photographs of Ferguson. There is 1 photograph of Maryann Mitchell.

Imagine the sheer indignation of the all-powerful Ferguson, that someone would commit such a heinous crime, murdering an innocent 16-year-old girl, in his own backyard. A young girl he knew. This case was personal, and it would be solved quickly. It had to be. And it would be he and his boys, not the investigators of Philadelphia homicide or Montgomery County detectives, who would have everything to do with solving it. To this end, a headquarters was established in the Philadelphia Fire Training School adjoining the Fifth District Police Station at Ridge Avenue and Cinnaminson Street.

Of primary importance to Fergie's Boys was establishing a scenario of what happened to Maryann once she left Koller's Kitchen. Frank Talbot was the driver that evening, he was asked by investigators if Maryann had gotten onto the bus as her friends had assumed she had. Talbot said, *"She did not, no one boarded the bus at Henry and Walnut Lane that evening."* Driver Jim Simpson was also questioned to ascertain if Maryann boarded the "Z" bus at Ridge and Leverington. Simpson verified that she had not. With this information, it was assumed that Maryann was abducted at the bus stop on Henry Avenue prior to the arrival of the "A" bus. The story began to be woven: The story that would match the confession down to the smallest detail.

Chapter 5: Mary Ann Comes Home

Sunday January 3, 1960

At 3:00 pm the body of Mary Ann was brought home to DuPont Street by funeral director John J. Modzianowski. The Mitchells had taken down the Christmas tree to *"Make room for our little angel"*, said a heartbroken Sarah Mitchell. As was the custom, the viewing was in the home. As Maryann's body was being laid out in the tiny living room, Sara Mitchell could be heard sobbing loudly upstairs. The public viewing that evening was from 5:30 to 9:00 pm. Police and detectives were there as if they half expected the murderer to turn up among the crowd of an estimated 3,000 relatives, friends and the curious who viewed the body of the slain schoolgirl.

Maryann was laid out in a white, ballerina style, chiffon gown, with full skirt and lace at the neck and shoulders. A white rosary was placed in Maryann's left hand and on her third finger was the amethyst ring she was wearing when she was killed. On her right wrist, which was badly bruised, was a corsage of white orchids. On the ring finger of her left hand was her high school ring. The casket was decked with flowers, two floral pillows of white carnations, lilies and gladioli at the head and foot. They bore the inscription "Our Daughter" in gold letters on a white banner.

Monday January 4, 1960

At 9 am a solemn requiem mass was celebrated for Maryann at Saint Josaphat Roman Catholic Church. Six young friends and neighborhood boys carried the coffin containing her body the short distance from the Mitchell home to the church. Mr. and Mrs. Mitchell followed behind the coffin. Edgar Mitchell had to literally hold his wife up in his arms, as she could barely walk she was so overcome with grief. Classmates from Cecilian Academy lined the street wearing round, white mantas upon their heads. The classmates stood side-by-side with the members of Maryann's Girl Scout troop.

The Reverend Charles Stelmach, curate of the church was the main celebrant. Reverend Richard Farrant, assistant pastor of Saint John the Baptist Church and Reverend Sebastian Babiarz of Saint Josaphat were con-celebrants.

At 3:05 pm that same day, a 39 year old man named Elmo Smith, a resident of Bridgeport, is apprehended at the Lafayette Motel in King of Prussia, PA by four Philadelphia detectives of the Special Investigation Squad: Emil Muller of South Philadelphia; Allen Hersh of South Philadelphia; George Gill of Tioga and Ronald Votter of Manayunk.

It wasn't much of an apprehension. Elmo Smith, along with his mother Flossie Smith, worked at the Motel. Elmo Smith was a convicted criminal on probation. One of the provisions of his probation was that he was not permitted to drive. His mother drove him to work each day. Mrs. Smith was on the housekeeping staff and Elmo was a handyman at the motel. The designated work unit for the handyman at the Motel was unit 101.

At the time he was confronted, Smith was changing fuses. Detective Muller was the first to approach Smith. Initially he ignored Muller telling him to, *"Wait a minute".* When Muller became emphatic, Smith stopped what he was doing and walked toward Muller. He was immediately taken by the detectives to the temporary task force headquarters at the Fire Training School and interrogated for 10 straight hours until 1:00 am the next morning by Fergie's boys.

Ferguson did not bother to notify Montgomery County investigators that they had a suspect in custody. He was convinced that the murder had occurred in his jurisdiction, Philadelphia. The body was then dumped in Montgomery County.

Upper Merion authorities complained that the detectives should have first consulted or advised them before taking the suspect from Montgomery County into

Philadelphia. They said they did not learn of Smith's apprehension until several hours later.

Later that evening Fergie's boys escorted Smith by car to the Roxy Theatre, Koller's Kitchen, and the Andorra Country Diner at Ridge Avenue and Sunset Street (another possible route location), for identification by staff and patrons. According to Ferguson's boys, several persons said they recognized the Bridgeport man as having frequented the premises. There would be no courtroom testimony to back up such witness identifications.

That same evening, in what is considered by some to be the biggest break in the investigation, a phone call was made to police headquarters in Bridgeport. Mrs. Peggy Grant of 710 Green Street reported a prowler had thrown a stone and struck her as she was walking to her home. Patrolman Thomas DeWan, sent to investigate, found no trace of a prowler. What officer DeWan did find was a cream and copper color Chevrolet BelAir sedan that fit the physical description of a car that had been reported stolen from Norristown on December 12, 1959. The plate on this car was stolen from a car registered in Coatesville, Pennsylvania.

The finding of that sedan would have absolutely no bearing on the murder of Maryann Mitchell unless certain events had transpired to make the car relevant. And here is where the theory begins.

Chapter 6: Thomas Bryson

In this theory, Thomas Bryson plays a paramount role in the arrest of Elmo Smith for the murder of Maryann. At the time, Thomas Bryson was the soon-to-be ex-husband of the woman Elmo Smith was dating in

December of 1959, twenty-seven year old Janet Bryson. Smith identified Janet Bryson as, *"My girlfriend since childhood".* Imagine the rage, or perhaps the fear, Thomas Bryson felt when he learned that his ex-wife was dating a convicted criminal who was on parole for a series of violent crimes against women. At the time of the murder, Janet Bryson lived with her parents in Lancaster County, Thomas Bryson resided in Coatesville.

It is believable, though not documented, that Thomas Bryson could have attempted to get Elmo Smith away from his ex-wife. To do so, Bryson could have set Smith up for a minor crime such as a robbery. On December 12, 1959 such a crime did take place in Norristown, Montgomery County. On that evening Theresa and Joseph Briggs attended a Christmas Party at the Knights of Columbus which was located two properties from their apartment at 825 Swede Street. They had walked to the party. At approximately 11:00 pm firefighters were dispatched to the Briggs apartment. A series of small fires had been set in the apartment. After the fires were extinguished the Briggs' entered the apartment to discover that items were missing including, among other things, a ladies wristwatch, which was broken. It is notable that Theresa Briggs stated that *"there were Christmas gifts in the apartment"*, but, the thief took a broken watch from her jewelry box? Also missing was the Briggs' 1958 cream and coco colored Chevrolet, BelAir sedan which had been parked in front of the apartment.

Could not Thomas Bryson have set the fires, stolen the watch, taken the car keys and stole the car? It was easy. The key to the car had been left in the apartment since Theresa and Joseph Briggs walked to the party. All that remained was for Bryson to connect the crime to Elmo Smith and Smith would be out of his ex-wife's life.

Initially, as the theory goes, that was Thomas Bryson's sole intention.

I have questioned many times if Thomas Bryson targeted the Briggs home randomly. Bryson worked at the Lukens Steel Plant in Coatesville, Joseph Briggs was a tool and die maker. Is there the possibility, that since their industries were related, they might, have been in the same place at the same time, perhaps at the Lukens Steel Plant? If so, Thomas Bryson could have been aware of Theresa and Joseph Briggs' plans to attend the Christmas party that evening and that their apartment would be empty, an ideal scenario for his intensions.

Again, in theory, Thomas Bryson took the car to Coatesville and changed the plates. At some point he drove the car to The Lafayette Motel where Smith was employed. He left the car unlocked with the stolen items in clear view, like bait. He returned to Coatesville via public transportation with the keys to the BelAir. Bryson's bet was that Smith would, at some point, notice the car parked for a prolonged period of time in the lot of the Motel. Upon inspection, and seeing the car unlocked, Bryson hoped that Smith, with his criminal background, would steal the contents thus guaranteeing a connection between the arson and robbery to Smith directly.

In the theory, the plan worked. Smith took the bait. He took the watch from the car, and as Thomas Bryson found out, Smith gave the watch to Janet Bryson as a Christmas gift. That was an added extra in Bryson's plan. Imagine the significant satisfaction Bryson felt when he asked Janet where she had gotten the watch she was wearing after Christmas: *"Elmo gave it to me",* she replied. All that remained was for Thomas Bryson to tip the police off that Elmo Smith had committed the crime at the Briggs home and that the stolen vehicle could be found at Elmo

Smith's place of employment the General Lafayette Motel in King of Prussia. It was easy. Bryson had committed the perfect frame-up of Elmo Smith.

Events would play out in a few short days that would escalate Thomas Bryson's plan to include an assurance of having Smith accused of murder. Surely, by the time Thomas Bryson was done, even his ex-wife and Elmo Smith's own mother Flossie would believe that Elmo Smith was guilty of murder. That too would be easy.

Thomas Bryson surely read the newspaper headlines that abounded on December 31, *"Police See Slaying as Work of Maniac"* and that "*Police are investigating the possibility that the killer might be the same person who attacked Joyce Davis on December 18, 1959 and had escaped in a light color sedan."* As the theory goes, Thomas Bryson, once again, returned to The General Lafayette Hotel, took the Briggs car, drove the car to Bridgeport and parked it on Green Street within a block of the rented home Elmo Smith shared with his parents.

Although Captain Ferguson and his boys claimed to have questioned hundreds of suspects and followed-up on as many tips and leads, and that Smith was caught as a result of a relentless manhunt and intense investigative work, it is more believable that Elmo Smith was delivered to Ferguson and his boys by a phoned in tip. In the theory, that source was Thomas Bryson and the information he disclosed was that Elmo Smith, a convicted felon, on parole only 3 months, for theft and brutal offences against 5 women, had given Janet Bryson a wristwatch that was stolen in a recent Norristown robbery on Swede Street.

And if the finding of the stolen BelAir appeared to be a lucky break, it was not what it appeared to be. In the theory it was Thomas Bryson who threw the stone to get police to the stolen car parked in unbelievably close proximity to Smith's residence.

The BelAir was locked when found by Patrolman DeWan. Immediately Police Chief Orfio Colliluori, State Troopers Herbert Hoffman and Chester Krupiewski went to the Green Street location. Colliluori called Samuel Pizza, owner of an auto service center at 1021 Ford Street in Bridgeport. Pizza forced a wire coat hanger through the window molding on the front door and tripped the lock. When opened, it was reported that blood was found on the back seat and on the inside panels of the rear doors. On the rear floor was found a nickel, a bobby pin and the top from a tube of lipstick. The interior dome light was shattered.

Tuesday January 5, 1960

The car was towed to Pizza's garage and Philadelphia authorities were called. Chief Detective Inspector John J. Kelly, Inspector George Kroubar, Captain Ferguson and Lt. Waters went to Bridgeport where they were joined by Montgomery County District Attorney Bernard DiJoseph at about 1:30 in the morning.

In the presence of both Philadelphia and Montgomery County authorities the car's trunk was broken open. Inside police found a 30 inch long upright portion of a bumper jack, a spare tire and a small Sunday missal used at Catholic Masses. And a document signed by Joseph Briggs.

The removable back seat of the car was pushed forward from its base, indicating that perhaps there had been a struggle. More bloodstains were found on the back of the seat and on the roof, just above the rear door.

There were also a few bloodstains on the front floorboards. An empty, crumpled cigarette pack was found at the base of the steering column.

Philadelphia crime laboratory technicians spent 3 hours going over the car inch-by-inch taking blood samples and fingerprints. They are said to have found three strands of auburn hair taken off the jack that were *"similar in all characteristics"* to Maryann's hair. Blood on the jack was identified as type "A" as were the bloodstains on the seat and floor of the car. Maryann had type "A" blood: The second most common blood type of Caucasians in America.

The lead technician who handled the evidence in this homicide was Agnes Mallatratt Douglas. Her boss was Dr. Edward Burke. Like Inspector Ferguson, Douglas was something of a local celebrity. In the least she was a memorable character. In the early 1960's she was profiled in the Philadelphia Inquirer as a *"Lab Sleuth"* and in The Bulletin as a *"Nemesis of Criminals"*. She was a favorite of police and prosecutors because she would find evidence against a suspect that others missed. She won several awards for her work.

In a November 28, 2010 in a Philadelphia Inquirer article, written by Fay Flam which related to Agnes Mallatratt Douglas, Flam cautions, "*Bias creeps in when investigators and crime lab technicians see themselves as working for just one side",* as indeed would seem to be the case in this investigation.

At 2:30 am Captain Clarence Ferguson stated emphatically to the Press, *"We have the murderer and we will get a conviction".* The case is turned over to Montgomery County District Attorney Bernard DiJoseph. Later that day Smith was transported from the Ridge and Cinnaminson Street location in Philadelphia to Norristown Prison in Montgomery County.

Chapter 7: Innocent Until Proven Guilty?

Wednesday: January 6, 1960

"Smith positively is the man who killed Maryann Mitchell. I am not 100 percent sure, I am a million percent sure Smith is guilty!" Ferguson assured the community. *"We will get a conviction".* With this mindset being proclaimed to the public, Elmo Smith never had a chance at innocence. He was found guilty by Ferguson. Back in '60 it was as if God himself had judged the man. Because Ferguson said it was so: SO IT WAS! There would, in reality, be no need for a trial.

On this day the man would be made to fit the crime. Joyce Ann Davis was taken to Norristown and identified Smith as the man who had stabbed her. Keep in mind, that when the assault occurred, Miss. Davis described her attacker as being *"about seventeen".* Smith was a, worn looking, 39 year old man with a receding hairline.

Miss Davis further identified the two-tone car found in Bridgeport as the car in which her assailant fled. A car she initially described as being a *"light color sedan"*. There was never any mention of two colors in her initial description. From the beginning Ferguson had fueled the media with the expectation that the attacker of Miss. Davis was most likely the murderer of Maryann Mitchell. Ferguson stated, in a published <u>Review</u> interview, *"We have been breaking our backs looking for this sadistic teenager and the white car, ever since the December 18 cutting. Frankly, at the time we expected him to strike again"*. Joyce Davis was assured by the infallible Ferguson, that this was, with no doubt or uncertainty, the man who attacked her and murdered Maryann.

This same day, the guilt of Elmo Smith was solidified when the watch he had given to Janet Bryson, on December 27, 1959, was recovered from her by police. When asked where he had gotten the watch, and not wanting to incriminate himself for stealing it from the parked car at the Hotel, Smith stated that: While he was walking, he found the watch under a bridge in Conshohocken.

Smith himself did not realize that the informer had already told police that Smith had stolen the watch from the Briggs home and that he had given it to Janet Bryson. He was caught in a lie and that lie reinforced the belief of investigators and the public that everything he said from that point on was a lie and that he must, without doubt, be guilty of the murder of Maryann Mitchell.

At 3:00 pm Smith was placed in a second lineup in an endeavor to have three 12-year-old girls from Phoenixville, Pennsylvania identify him as the person who fled in an automobile after attempting to abduct them. There is no indication that the girls identified Smith. The girls did not testify at Smith's trial.

Thursday January 7, 1960

At 7:00 pm Smith requested to talk to his mother, Flossie Smith and Janet Bryson. At 8:30 pm the women arrive at Norristown Prison. After the visit, during which the women pleaded with Smith to confess if he committed the crime, it was reported in newspaper accounts that, *"Smith readily admitted to the murder and agreed to re-enact the crime"*. Yet, in court testimony the Chief of Montgomery County Detectives would testify that he heard Smith tell the women that, he knew nothing about the crime. By the end of this day there would be a seven page "confession" signed by Smith. Captain Ferguson and his Boys, by Ferguson's own account said, *"Smith was interrogated, relentlessly, day and night, for three days"*.

The Review reports in the January 7, 1960 edition, that on December 31 a missing piece of the garter belt was wearing, was uncovered in Bridgeport, but, not in the home of Elmo Smith. In that same edition it is reported in The Review that a pair of bloodstained shoes and new white socks, also bloodstained, were found in the Bridgeport home of Smith, but only after a "second search" of the apartment was done. Upon that search, the blood stained items were reportedly found in a waste basket.

There is never any mention of the keys to the stolen BelAir being found in either, Smith's apartment, work place or in the stolen BelAir. In his statement to Montgomery County Investigators, Elmo Smith stated that, *"I left the keys in the car when I parked it."* The keys are important yet, they were not presented as evidence at the trial. One must question: Why were the keys not presented? Would not those keys have had fingerprints on them? And if Elmo Smith was the driver of the car, the fingerprints would surely be his. Neither Elmo Smith, nor Maryann Mitchell's fingerprints were found in the stolen BelAir. Nor were Elmo Smith's fingerprints found on the bumper jack.

Friday January 8, 1960

Smith was returned to his Norristown Prison cell at 4:05 am after taking Montgomery County investigators on the route he supposedly took with Maryann. The same route he had been taken on by Fergie's boys on the evening of January 4, 1960.

Six hours later, at 10:00 am, Smith was arraigned at the Whitemarsh Township Building on Joshua Road. Smith was escorted into the room by detectives and State Troopers. His expression was blank and he kept almost perfectly still, except when he was addressed by Justice of the Peace Louis W. Hofman. He added "sir" to all of his answers and he calmly corrected Hofman when asked *"You are Elmo F. Smith?"* Smith replied, *"Elmo L. sir; L for Lee, sir"*. Hofman asked, *"Were you ever in trouble before"?* Smith answered quietly, *"Yes sir, in 1947"*. It was reported that Smith showed only a trace of what could be called emotion. Each time Hofman said "Maryann" and "murderer" the defendant closed his eyes slightly.

Smith pled guilty. These details were gleaned from the statement read by Police Chief Edgar Mitchell of Whitemarsh Township, who officially filed the information against Smith:

Shortly before 10:30 pm December 28, 1959 he saw Maryann waiting in the rain for a bus in Roxborough at Walnut Lane and Henry Avenue. He 'somehow' got her into his car. Instead of driving her home to 195 DuPont Street in Manayunk, Smith stopped the car 'somewhere' in Roxborough, overpowered the girl and raped her. Smith then drove to Conshohocken. On Spring Mill Avenue, between Eighth and Ninth Avenues, near the Hale Fire Pump Company, he attempted to rape her again. The girl resisted and Smith bludgeoned her with the bumper jack.

She was still alive and in a semi-conscious state when he transported her to Whitemarsh Township where he pulled the girl from the rear seat of the car and rolled her down the embankment on Harts Lane near Barren Hill. The girl pleaded with Smith to take her home, but he left her telling her, 'To hell with you, walk home'. He drove to Bridgeport and abandoned the car on Sixth Street.

He returned to his apartment and had a pleasant conversation with his mother. He said he stole the car in Norristown in the middle of December near a hotel, it contained: a purse in which was the wrist watch.

The content of the statement was no sooner released then the validity of it was questioned. Authorities tell the public, via the media, that they are inclined to believe Smith is lying about several aspects of the case.

Most inconsistent, the lapse of time from when Smith supposedly left Maryann in the ditch (11:30 pm Monday, December 28) and when her body was discovered (2:30 pm Wednesday, December 30) do not jibe with what was uncovered in the 'relentless investigation'. Was this a detailed confession of the actual events of December 28, 1959 by Elmo Smith to which he signed his name? Or, was this the scenario investigators developed regarding the events of December 28, 1959?

Who Is Elmo Smith?

Elmo Smith was born in Richmond, Virginia in 1921. He was a man of slight physical stature; he was 5 feet, 8 inches tall and weighed 145 pounds.

In a February 12, 1965 Delaware County, <u>Daily</u> <u>Times</u> interview with reporter Gretchen LaFleur, Flossie Smith described her son Elmo saying, *"He was a happy baby and always a good boy at home. I never found him telling me anything that wasn't true".*

Elmo Smith had one brother, his name was Melvin. According to his mother, Elmo was married at age 18 in 1939. When he married he converted to Catholicism. In 1941 Smith and his wife were living in Manayunk, he was employed as a truck driver. He served in the Army from August 12, 1942 until January 16, 1946 serving much of that time in Hawaii. He was honorably discharged in 1946. He and his wife moved into 623 Cherry Street in Bridgeport, PA. They had one son who was born in 1946. By 1949 they were divorced. My research indicates the Elmo Smith's wife re-married and his son was adopted by her second husband a resident of Norristown..

Beginning in 1946 there was a thirteen month string of break-ins in Montgomery County. The break-ins appeared to be sexually motivated with intent to assault. Women were observed by the male assailant from outside their homes, he would then enter the home. In some cases phone lines were cut prior to entry. On one occasion the female victim was severely assaulted with a rolling-pin. In a few of the break-ins the perpetrator was confronted by a family member of the would-be victim and would run out of the home. On one occasion, separate from the break-ins, a male exposed himself, naked from the waist down, on a public street. In each case the would-be perpetrator got away. The last of the assaults was on a snowy day, and the assailant fled in a car that had snow chains on the tires. The car tracks were traced to a garage on Cherry Street. Elmo Smith lived in the house next to the garage where the car was found. The string of break-ins, attempted assaults, assaults and attempted robberies reportedly ended with Elmo Smith's arrest for the crimes in January 1948. The car did not belong to Elmo Smith.

In 1948, Smith had pled guilty to five charges of aggravated assault and battery with intent to criminally assault and five charges of burglary. He was sentenced for a term of 10 to 20 years.

In 1950 Smith claimed that his confession was coerced and that he did not willingly plead guilty. He requested that he wanted a lawyer to appeal his conviction. A lawyer was not secured and Elmo Smith represented his self. Smith claimed that when he was brought in for questioning on January 4, 1948 he was not cooperative. He worried that his wife and son did not know where he was and that he wanted to go home. He claimed investigators tried to force a confession from him, *"Sergeant or Patrolman Hoffman of the State Police did all the punching and the slapping me in the face because I refused to answer questions".*

Elmo Smith then stated, *"I was taken to the Norristown State Hospital, given truth serum [sodium pentothal]. I was returned to city hall and told, I had confessed to all the crimes that were committed in the [Montgomery] Count. I was told I was going into court and plead guilty to them."* On January 5, 1948, at 1:10 am Smith signed a confession. The confession and his guilty plea were upheld in the 1950 hearing.

In regard to Smith's 1948 conviction, Flossie Smith, in the LaFleur <u>Daily</u> <u>Times</u> interview on February 12, 1950 Mrs. Smith is quoted as saying: *"We had recently moved to Bridgeport when he [Elmo] was first arrested for those crimes back in 1948. I couldn't believe it. Elmo was a stranger there. Some of the crimes they accused him of I didn't understand because when they were suppose to have happened he was with us. I'm not trying to excuse him, I just don't understand."*

Smith was released from prison in January of 1958 after serving 10 years of the 10-20 year sentence. The psychiatrist who examined Smith just before he was released from prison documented, *"He appears well oriented in all spheres…no evidence of memory defects or confusion and no significant abnormalities".*

Upon his release in January 1959 he worked on the farm of Dewey Schrider, a longtime family friend and the father of Janet Bryson. Wanting to work with cars he wrote a letter on March 1, 1958 to the Lancaster Malleable Casting Company seeking employment, a portion of the letter reads, *"I always worked steady and never been fired from any job, always left to better myself to something better".*

In June of 1959, Elmo Smith was back in jail. He had gotten a driver's license and that was a violation of his parole. In October of 1959, Elmo Smith was once again released from prison. He went home to live with his parents in Bridgeport. Unable to drive, he secured a job as a handyman at the Lafayette Motel in King of Prussia where his mother worked and she would drive him to and from work each day.

Flossie Smith, in the same LaFleur, <u>Daily</u> <u>Times</u> interview of February 12, 1960, gives an account of

Elmo's days on December 28 and 29,1959: *"Elmo left the house around 8 [pm] Monday and said he was going to a movie. He came home around 20 minutes to 12 [midnight]; I know because I keep a clock on the desk in the bedroom. He said he was home and came upstairs to bed. The next morning he got up just like he always does at 6:45[am], came downstairs and got washed. He helped me get breakfast ready. We sat and talked while he ate three eggs, bacon and toast and milk. Then we left for work so we'd be on time. We worked all day. He and I drove home together like we always do and when we got home he and my husband, it was his day off, went out to the workshop. We had dinner and they went back out to the workshop and worked some more. Then we sat around the table and watched some television and had something to eat. We went to bed Tuesday night around 11 o'clock. The next day [Wednesday] the same thing happened and everything was just as usual".*

It was after his release in October that Elmo started going out with Janet Bryson. She was separated from her husband. Flossie Smith was worried about them dating believing that Elmo would be violating his parole. Flossie Smith advised Janet and Elmo that they should not see one another until after Janet's divorce from Thomas Bryson was final. The advice fell on deaf ears.

Paul Garnet, Chairman of the State Parole Board and a former Bucks County warden stated that, *"Our parole officer visited his [Elmo's] parents, his employer and a prospective new employer as late as December 22, 1959 and found no sign that anything was wrong".*

Smith, along with his mother was a member of the Bridgeport Baptist Church. Rev. John H. Walker, the pastor, said *"Since his release from prison Elmo and his mother attended church every Sunday. December 27th was no different; Elmo and his mother attended Church and received communion. There was no indication that anything was wrong."*

Wednesday January 13, 1960

Joyce Davis was assigned around-the-clock police protection as the result of receiving a threatening letter which read: *"Beware, you are next. I will get you for lying on Smith. He is not the man who stabbed you in your arm. I am. The next time I will not try to knife you. You will get the same thing I gave Maryann Mitchell. Elmo Smith is not the man they want. I am. I am still free to kill. I will get you as soon as I can."* The envelope was post marked in Philadelphia.

Thursday January 14, 1960

A plethora of articles were published in the January 14, 1960 edition of The Review concerning the murder of Maryann and boosting the ego of Clarence Ferguson. Featured on the front page alone there were five stories.

The right half of the front page is divided into two columns the first headline reads:

"You're Next 'Killer' Tells Joyce Davis" in this article the content of the letter is printed.

To the right of that column the headline is **"Elmo Smith Is Calm At Confession, Plea Of Guilt Causes Stir"**.

The top center of the newspaper shows a captioned photo **"BIGGEST MAN IN POLICE WORK**…*Captain Clarence J. Ferguson, is acclaimed 'biggest man in police work in the whole United States of America' by Judge Adrian Bonnelly, president judge of Philadelphia Municipal Court, as latter awards B'Nai Zion Lodge 23 plaque for dedicated performance of duty Nov. 30 at Palumbo's. Adding his tribute is Col. Frank G. McCartney, State Police Commissioner. Ferguson, McCartney collaborated in solving Maryann Mitchell Murder"*. This same photo had appeared in the December 3, 1959 edition of The Review .

Directly below the captioned photo of Ferguson, in the center of the front page, in bold letters, the title of the article reads: **"Weekly Review Papers First To Spotlight Police Ability"**. The article reads in portion: *"The metropolitan daily newspapers and Montgomery County's Norristown Daily carried editorials on Saturday lauding Captain Clarence J. Ferguson for his brilliant work in speedily solving the savage sex murder of Maryann Mitchell. The Sunday papers were lavish in their praise of the Upper Roxborough resident. They affectionately called him a 'cop's cop'. Throughout the investigation this newspaper received time and again exclusive stories on the case from Captain Ferguson and members of his Special Investigation Squad. When praise began flowing in Captain Ferguson's direction some nice things were said that we wished we had said first. And then we remembered we had said them first! Weekly Review papers were forwarded yesterday to Captain Ferguson's long time friend Jimmy Durante, at his home* *in Beverly Hills where the captain and his wife, Rosalind, were guests of 'The Schnoz' early in December".*

Next to this article, we see for the first time, the face of Elmo Smith. It is one-third the size of the Clarence J. Ferguson photo that appears above it. It is now all about the brilliance of Ferguson as an "investigator". There are no photographs of Maryann on the page.

On the bottom left of the page there is a short article titled **"In Youth, Remember…"** In that story, startling information is revealed concerning public opinion in regard to Elmo Smith:

"Teenagers are finding themselves mightily restricted since the savage murder of Maryann Mitchell, and families requiring baby-sitters are having a tough time getting anybody. There is a feeling terror lurks everywhere. And yet in the midst of recognizing the brutality of the indignities and the blows inflicted on the 16-year-old Manayunk girl there are many, many people who keep saying, 'Is Elmo Smith really guilty'? Some have gone so far as to suggest the Bridgeport convict was framed by police! This attitude is an amazing mass reaction. Why sympathy for a criminal for whom prison doors never should have been opened by parole in the first place, due to the number and magnitude of previous offenses he committed?"

Next to this article is a photo of the 4 detectives who "apprehended" Smith. The caption on the photograph reads: "**ELMO SMITH FEARED THEM**- *'I'd confessed sooner, but I was afraid they'd tear me to pieces,' Elmo Smith supposedly said, after pleading guilty Friday to clobbering Maryann Mitchell to death. At a hearing in the Whitemarsh Township Building: Detectives, Allen Hersh, Ronald S. Votto, Emil Mueller and George Gill* who apprehended Smith. *Yesterday disappointed that court refused to call a special session of Grand Jury, Smith threatened to repudiate confession."*

In this same edition on page 7, a sixth article is published: **"Did Slayer Plant Clues for Police To Capture Him?"** Segments of the article are as follows: *"Considerable pressure was brought from various sources favoring Smith's release for lack of evidence. But Ferguson put his 42 years of experience on the line. 'That's the man" he insisted, again and again."* In this article, the lipstick scrawlings the killer drew on Maryann's body are mentioned, *"While there is considerable speculation as to the meaning of the initials "TB" and " 101", the unofficial consensus seemed to be that Smith, realizing he could not control his sex impulses, wanted to be captured and imprisoned before he struck again. 'T' is the 20th letter of the alphabet, 'B' the second letter. That would be 202. The motel is on route 202 and 23. The room he occupied bore the number 101. The arc connecting the letters and numerals may have roughly indicated a turnpike interchange."* The article ends with mention of the stolen car: *"The manner in which he [Smith] abandoned the stolen automobile, used in the murder, and discarded pieces of garments and other things belonging to Maryann Mitchell also indicate that he deliberately had a hand in tightening the net in which he is now firmly held as Maryann's slayer."*

That January 14, 1960 edition of The Review ends with two final pieces related to the homicide. On page 12, the back page of the paper there is an article captioned **"Capt. Ferguson Home to Breakfast; Had to Eat on Run in Murder Probe"** it reads in part: *"Captain Clarence J. Ferguson sat down to breakfast in his home at 612 Crestview Rd., Upper Roxborough, and had his first leisurely meal, Monday morning. Mrs. Ferguson*

gave the head of the Philadelphia investigating squad his
normal breakfast of: a whole grapefruit, one fried egg,
toast and two cups of coffee. Mrs. Ferguson pointed out
that her husband now only eats one egg at the morning
meal, 'He used to eat two or three but now he's cutting
down'. She said that his real favorite at breakfast is
grapefruit." At the end of that three column article
Ferguson shares his six reasons for holding Elmo Smith
for the murder of Maryann: *"There were human*
scratches on Smith's back. There was blood under the
nails of four fingers of his right hand. Blood was found
on his shoes. His bloodstained coat had been sent to the
cleaner. The people at 9282 Ridge Avenue who found
Maryann's purse described the brown-and-cream
Chevrolet they had seen. Smith gave three different
stories about his movements on the night of the murder.
Each one turned out to be false."

Chapter 8: The Pieces Aren't Fitting

Again, by January 26, 1960 investigators
acknowledged that there were inconsistencies in Elmo
Smith's 'confession' and the forensic evidence: Drastic
inconsistencies. Whitemarsh Township Police Chief
Mitchell stated clearly that he does not believe Smith's
account that he struck the girl after he attempted to rape
her a second time on Spring Mill Avenue in
Conshohocken, while they were in the stolen car.

Philadelphia Pathologist Marvin Aronson said that he
agrees with Montgomery County coroner Dr. John
Simpson that death occurred within minutes after the fatal
blows and that the body was found ten hours after death
occurred. Maryann died early Wednesday morning close

to 2:30 am, there was no possibility she was beaten on Monday evening.

Dr. Aronson stated that the hamburger in Maryann's stomach was eaten about 2 hours before her death. If it had been eaten earlier it would have been digested.

There was one final puzzling piece of forensic evidence, a pickle was found in Maryann's stomach. When Maryann and her friends went to Koller's and ate, her friends agreed that Maryann did not eat a pickle.

The possibility now presented itself: Could Maryann have been given a hamburger at a later time, possibly by her killer? Was Maryann a captive for a day?

Strong rumblings by the public and investigators alike began to be heard in Philadelphia and Montgomery County questioning the guilt of Smith. The 'confession' was all wrong. Perhaps Ferguson had the wrong guy.

If there was a "Good Old Boys Club" in the suburbs of Philadelphia in the 50's and 60's two charter members were Clarence Ferguson and Harold McCuen, the two fueled one another's passions: Ferguson to be in the news and McCuen to report the news.

Harold McCuen was somewhat of a Suburban Media Man. In 1948 he formed the Weekly Review Publishing Company which published several newspapers, including the <u>Roxborough</u> <u>Review</u>, the <u>Chestnut</u> <u>Hill</u> <u>Herald</u>, the <u>Valley</u> <u>Forge</u> <u>Sentinel</u> the <u>Leader-Review</u> and the <u>Suburban</u> <u>Press</u>. McCuen was a personal friend of Clarence Ferguson. And Ferguson was very often the subject of McCuen's newspaper stories. What better friend for a media hound to have than the multi-faceted reporter, photographer, columnist, editor and publisher of newspapers.

On January 22, in response to the rumblings of, Ferguson having caught the wrong guy and the possibility of Elmo Smith's innocence, Harold McCuen wrote and published this seething Editorial in <u>The</u> <u>Review</u>:

Hero Worship For Girl's Slayer

"Two weeks after Elmo Smith's confession to the sadistic murder of a 16-year-old Manayunk girl, sympathy continues mounting today for the 39-year-old convicted criminal who committed the murder while he was on a parole that never should have been granted. What magnetic power does Elmo Smith possess? Why are intelligent people, including mothers, referring to him as 'Poor Elmo' and continuing to regard to him as a suspect, rather than the confessed slayer he is? Public opinion in favor of the paroled convict is one of the most amazing reactions this editor has witnessed in his 35 years in journalism. Most men and women who mention the case express doubt that Smith is guilty, that he committed the crime unaided by a second party, that his crime, horrible in every respect, does not merit a death penalty! They should have been present during the autopsy performed in a Conshohocken funeral home. They should have accompanied the crew of four men from the Whitemarsh Township highway department that found Maryann's clobbered body in a gully on the afternoon of Wednesday, December 30. Described as a 'quiet, mild-mannered person,' Elmo Smith possesses a dynamic personality. He packs a powerful wallop, a deadly blow, when it suits his purpose. His powerful punch felled a parole board of three, a judge and a district attorney. They set him free after he served 10 years of a 20 year

sentence, turned him loose even after breaking parole and moved extremely slowly into investigating a complaint regarding a second violation of his parole just a week or two before he snatched Maryann Mitchell while she was waiting for a bus at 10:20 P.M. Monday, December 28, at Walnut Lane and Henry Avenue, Roxborough. A quiet, mild-mannered man! What became of his quiet, mild-mannered disposition when he had a defenseless 16-year-old girl in his clutches, a girl weighing 110 pounds? What savage blows he inflicted with a bumper jack upon her skull! A brave man, this Elmo, with helpless victims, but quiet, mild-mannered in the presence of husky State Troopers armed with pistol and blackjack. Is it dynamic personality or diabolical genius? Smith quietly requested that the Montgomery County District Attorney go into court and ask for a speedy trial. And the District Attorney obliged! Fortunately, four judges weren't impressed. Apparently, there's nothing we can do to convince anybody that Elmo Smith deserves no sympathy. We said in an editorial on January 7, the day before Smith's confession was made known, that the hottest place in hell is reserved for him. It is. We sincerely hope, however, that the details we have published regarding this sordid crime will have a tendency to warn all teenagers to be on guard against quiet, mild-mannered men capable of fooling adults even when they have a prison record and are at large on parole. It is significant that widespread sympathy, even defensive adoration, of a sex degenerate should exist. The public seemingly wants to be as soft toward criminals as the parole-board and the pardon-board are known to be in Pennsylvania".

Chapter 9: Pre-Trial Tid Bits

Thursday February 4, 1960

In early January Ferguson claimed that, *"The apprehension of Smith resulted from questioning hundreds of suspects and following-up on as many tips and leads, and that Smith was caught as a result of a relentless manhunt and intense investigative work"*. On this day, while speaking at a noon, Roxborough-Manayunk Lions Club Meeting, Ferguson admits: *"The apprehension of Smith was the result of a tip from an informer"*.

Thursday March 10, 1960

At 8:30 A.M. Smith is taken from the County Prison to the Court House on Swede Street in Norristown to appear before the Grand Jury. Smith is guarded by 10 deputy sheriffs as the result of a rumor that someone was going to shoot him. He was handcuffed to Deputy Sheriff Morton Bailey of Flourtown and surrounded by the other deputies on the short walk from the Prison to the Court House. Attorneys Gilbert P. High and Joseph P. Phelps, court-appointed to represent Smith at the Grand Jury arraignment only were by his side. It was stated at that time that two other attorneys will be named to represent Smith if the case goes to trial.

Edwin Mitchell, Maryann's father, was in the courtroom and kept his eyes glued on Smith. Judge David E. Groshens presided at the arraignment. District Attorney Bernard DiJoseph read the bill of indictment which charges Smith with Maryann's murder.

The Grand Jury heard evidence offered by Whitemarsh chief of police Edgar Mitchell, chief of Montgomery

County detectives Charles Moody, State Police captain George Sauer, State Police sergeant Herbert Hoffman, Montgomery County coroner Dr. John Simpson, Philadelphia homicide squad detective Samuel Hammes, Bridgeport chief of police Orfio Collilouri and Norristown chief of police Robert Baxter. Clarence J. Ferguson was not at the hearing. Neither Clarence Ferguson, nor the detectives of the Philadelphia Special Investigation Unit offered evidence or testimony.

After a two hour deliberation the Grand Jury found a true bill on the charge of murder. The trial is expected to be scheduled for June.

Thursday March 24, 1960

It is announced that defense attorneys Gilbert High and Joseph Phelps will represent Smith at trial. The appointment of the attorneys was the result of a petition filed by District Attorney Bernard DiJoseph after Smith pleaded "no funds or indigence" and therefore was unable to retain legal counsel. The appointment was sanctioned by all four Montgomery County judges, Judge William F. Dannehower, Judge E. Arnold Forrest, Judge David E. Groshens and Judge Robert W. Honeymat.

Monday March 28, 1960

A young, expectant, mother is attacked at knifepoint at the McDevitt Playground located on 3531 Scott's Lane in East Falls. The location is approximately 2.5 miles from where Joyce Davis was attacked and approximately 1 mile South on Henry Avenue from where Maryann was last seen.

The woman was at the playground with her 2-year-old daughter when the assailant suddenly approached wielding a knife. He agreed to leave the child alone after the mother pleaded with him. She was assaulted in the woods adjacent to the playground. He told her, "Don't make a sound or I'll cut your throat". He then let her go.

When she returned to the playground, her daughter was there wandering around and crying. She took the child home and phoned police. She was later taken to the hospital of the Woman's Medical College.

She described the attacker as a white man about 25-years-old, with a freckled face. He was about 5 feet, nine inches tall and weighed about 140 pounds. He was wearing a light colored plaid shirt and faded blue dungarees.

Could the attacker of Joyce Davis and this attacker be one and the same? Could the identification by Joyce Davis of Elmo Smith have been wrong? Also, is it possible that this attacker authored the threatening note written to Miss. Davis?

Elmo Smith never once, in each of the 5 assaults for which he was convicted, used a knife, nor was a knife used in the Maryann Mitchell homicide.

In an April 1960 edition of the magazine Official Detective Stories the cover is featured with the caption "The Full Story Behind Philadelphia's Maryann Mitchell Slaying". It is a seven page article written by Al Richards, Special Investigator for Actual Detective Stories. The pages contain 16 photographs related to the murder of Maryann. On page 23 of the magazine it is stated that Clarence Ferguson asked Constance Kerns and Mary Ann Carney *"Where did sh e[Maryann] wait for the bus?"* They replied *"At Henry Avenue and Walnut Lane"*, the article goes on further to state that; *"Constance and Mary Ann had seen Maryann cross Henry Avenue to the bus stop. They saw a bus approaching but they hadn't stopped to watch Maryann get on"*.

In the article Al Richards reports further, *"Questioning of attendants at a service station next to the diner [Koller's Kitchen] likewise revealed no clue. Although the station was across the street from the bus stop, no one had seen the victim or heard any screams. Interrogation of bus drivers and employees of the Roxy Theater produced nothing. None of the theater personnel could help them, nor could any of the drivers on the routes she would have taken remember seeing a girl of her [Maryann's] description that night"*.

Saturday April 9, 1960

In an address which Clarence Ferguson delivers at the Annual Activities Banquet at North Light Boys Club in Manayunk, his sheer ego-centric arrogance is revealed: *"I was proud that it was I and my men who tracked down Elmo Smith, placed him under arrest and led to his confession of the crime. It was not easy to solve the Mitchell murder. We had very little evidence to work on. We received little or no cooperation from Montgomery County authorities and none from the District Attorney, there. I am sorry to have to say that we got very little cooperation or encouragement from some of our own Philadelphia Police officials. But I have been a policeman for many years and I have learned that when there is a job to do you do it. Besides, I had a personal interest. The Mitchell family, were friends of my family"*.

Tuesday April 12, 1960

Montgomery County District Attorney Bernard DiJoseph is found slumped over the wheel of his Volkswagen at the intersection of Church and Paper Mill Roads. The prosecutor's car was at a standstill, first in line at the traffic light. He was transported to Abington Memorial hospital where he was pronounced dead of an apparent heart attack. Mr. DiJoseph was 51 years old.

Back in January, after Elmo Smith's arraignment DiJoseph went into court to request a speedy trial for Smith. The district attorney's request, entered on behalf of Smith, was denied. Later, in answer to criticism as to why Mr. DiJoseph apparently placed himself in the position of offering to help a confessed sex killer, the district attorney said *"Smith felt the DA was the only friend he had". "But"*, the district attorney explained, *"You can be assured I will do everything in my power to get a conviction of murder in the first degree, when this case goes to trial".*

In the same issue and article that announces the death of district attorney DiJoseph, Harold McCuen applauds his friend, Captain Ferguson for having two articles on the Mitchell murder case published in two detective magazines that have nation-wide circulation.

Ferguson anxiously awaits a subpoena to testify at the much anticipated trial. He would never receive one.

Monday June 24, 1960

Announcement was made by Montgomery County President Judge William F. Dannehower that the Smith trial will be held in Gettysburg. The announcement was made upon reception of an order decided upon by the

State Supreme Court of Pennsylvania and issued by Chief Justice Alvin Jones. President Judge, Honorable W. Clarence Sheely will be the trial judge. The jury will be composed of residents from Adams County. The trial will begin on August 23, 1960.

The decision to transfer the case to Adams County was reached by the full Court. The high court was requested to decide the site after a hearing on June 16 before the Judges of Montgomery County Court on Smith's petition for a change of venue.

In the petition, Smith's attorneys stated, *"The prisoner cannot obtain a fair trial in Montgomery County or adjoining counties because of widespread publicity the case has received."*

Thursday August 18, 1960

Smith's court appointed attorneys disclosed Smith will repudiate his confession when he takes the stand in Gettysburg.

Chapter 10: The Trial

Assistant district attorney Anthony Cirillo became lead prosecutor in the case following the sudden death of district attorney Bernard DiJoseph. Both DiJoseph and Cirillo had worked on the case together. Cirillo is being assisted by assistant district attorney Richard Bixby.

Elmo Smith pleads not guilty. But it is already too late. As stated in The Journal of Credibility Assessment and Witness Psychology 1999, Vol. 2, No. 1, 14-36

"The introduction of a confession makes the other aspects of a trial in court superfluous, and the real trial, for all practical purposes, occurs when the confession is obtained"

Tuesday August 23, 1960

As the trial begins in Gettysburg, it is published in <u>The</u> <u>Review</u> that the detectives of the special investigation squad of the Philadelphia police department will claim all the reward offered for the arrest of the murderer of Maryann Mitchell.

Wednesday August 24, 1960

In a 12 minute opening address, assistant district Attorney Cirillo described the charges against Smith. He stated that robbery was the motive for the crime. Robbery and criminal assault are felonies and a murder committed during the commission of a felony is first degree murder under the law, punishable by life in prison or death.

Cirillo said that the Commonwealth would prove that Smith: *"Slugged Maryann with a bumper jack and dragged her into a car which was stolen; drove her from Philadelphia to Conshohocken, throwing her clothing out a window as he went; parked and attacked her and viciously beat her again over the head several times; drove to Whitemarsh Township and rolled her body down an embankment into a gully".*

Today, for the first time, the Commonwealth revealed that Maryann was struck down while she waited for a bus on Henry Avenue at Walnut Lane. That she had not gotten into a car willingly. Cirillo said, *"Smith sneaked up behind her and hit her over the head with the bumper jack and dragged her into a stolen car"*. This new angle was based on a thin bruise found behind one of Maryann's ears. *"The bruise was thin"*, Cirillo said, *Because she was standing under an umbrella when the blow was struck and the umbrella caved in as someone hit her with a heavy weapon"*. Cirillo stated further, *"There is reason to believe Maryann was unconscious when she was dragged into the sedan"*.

As the trial began, Mrs. Sarah Mitchell was the first of four prosecution witnesses to testify. For the first time she saw face-to-face the man accused of killing her daughter. She wept as she was asked to identify the blood stained clothing as having belonged to Maryann. Piece by piece, with heart-wrenching emotion, she confirmed each piece of the clothing evidence as belonging to, and having been worn by, Maryann on the evening she disappeared.

According to Mrs. Mitchell's testimony she said that the last time she saw her daughter Maryann was about 4 pm. She had a $1.00 bill in her purse for the movies. Sarah Mitchell returned home from her job at midnight to find that Maryann had not come home from the evening out with her friends. Sarah Mitchell phoned Mary Ann Carney who said that *"Maryann was getting on the 10:20 bus"*. At about 12:15 Sarah Mitchell phoned police to report her daughter missing. There was no cross examination of Sarah Mitchell by the defense.

Mr. Edwin Mitchell, the father of Maryann Mitchell was the next witness to testify. He identified the same clothing evidence as had his wife.

Mr. Mitchell testified for the prosecution that the last time he saw Maryann was at 5:30 on the evening of December 18, 1959. She had $2.00 in her purse before leaving for her Aunt Elizabeth Gillespie's house. He remembered her scotch taping one of the dollar bills together. In his court testimony Edwin Mitchell then stated that *"the last time I heard from Maryann was at 5:45, she was home getting dressed, she called me on the phone to tell me that my supper was on the range"*. He testified further that he returned home between 6:30 and 6:40.

Edwin Mitchell was then cross examined by the defense: He testified *"I left the house at 5:30 right after Dance Band [a T.V. Show] went off [the air] and went to the corner tap room. Maryann called me at 6:30 [pm] to tell me my dinner was on the stove"*.

Witness Elizabeth Gillespie, Maryann's great-aunt testified that Maryann and Sophie arrived at her home at 6:30 [pm]. There was no cross-examination by the defense of Elizabeth Gillespie.

Witness Sophie Sutch testified that, *"At 6:00 [pm] Maryann was getting ready to go out, she was putting packages in a brown bag [handbag] so they wouldn't get wet"*. Sophie testified that, *"We left her [Maryann's] Aunt's house to pick up Mary Ann Carney. We waited for Connie Kerns then all four of us left for the Roxy. At 6:45 we turned down a ride from four boys on the Ridge. We arrived at the Roxy at 7:30 [pm] to see South Pacific. We left the Roxy at 9:30 [pm]. I went home alone."*

There was no cross examination of Sophie Sutch by the defense.

Thursday August 25, 1960

Witness Constance Kerns, a student at Raven Hill Academy testified that following the movie, she, Maryann [Mitchell] and Mary Ann Carney walked to Koller's Kitchen. *"I last saw Maryann [Mitchell] about 300' from Koller's Kitchen about to cross Henry Avenue at Jamestown Street".* There is no testimony by Constance Kearns of *"seeing a bus approach as Maryann crossed Henry Avenue",* although that paramount detail was reported in initial interviews of Constance.

Mary Ann Carney, 16, testified she last saw Maryann alive as she was crossing Henry Avenue on her way to the bus stop. As well, there is no testimony by Mary Ann Carney of *"seeing the bus approach as Maryann crossed Henry Avenue"* as she had stated previously.

In Mary Ann's testimony from the trial transcripts, she stated that, *"Yes, Maryann [Mitchell] ate a pickle".* This statement contradicted her statement when she was initially questioned by investigators.

Saturday August 27, 1960

Janet Bryson testified that Smith gave her a watch, identified as stolen by Theresa Briggs, on December 27, 1959 the day before Maryann disappeared.

Dr. Edward Burke, city chemist for the Philadelphia Police Department testified that, Maryann Mitchell, from all indications of his tests, was never in the front seat of the 1958 Chevrolet BelAir believed to have been used by Smith.

Under cross examination by the defense however, Burke said, his tests, from all indications, showed that Smith had never been in the back seat of the car.

Cirillo submitted into evidence, hair found on the rear arm rest of the vehicle, hair from the head of Elmo Smith, hair from the head of Maryann Mitchell, and hair taken off the jack found in the rear of the car. Dr. Burke testified that his tests showed three types of hair in the car. Under cross examination by the defense he said, *"Hair is not classified like fingerprints, it can belong to any number of people"*. He testified that, *"Hairs found on the front seat of the stolen car are similar to those of Smith"*.

In regard to fiber evidence in the front seat, Burke said he *"Didn't look for fibers in the car to match those of the defendant"*. He added, that he was *"only trying to match the fibers with Maryann's clothing. None were found to match Miss. Mitchell's clothing"*. I could find no accounts of any fingerprints being entered into evidence at the trial. One is led to believe that the absence of such evidence indicates that the fingerprints of Elmo Smith were not found in either the stolen car or on the bumper jack. As well, by the absence of testimony, one is also led to believe that Maryann's fingerprints were not found in the car.

Leon Webster Metcher, a handwriting expert, testified that letters and numerals written, in lipstick, on Maryann's stomach exhibited handwriting similar to Smith's.

Next, Wayne Mowery, a gas station attendant in Norristown, was called as a witness for the prosecution. Mowery testified that on the evening of December 24, 1959 Smith drove into the gas station where he worked and ordered two-dollars worth of gasoline. Smith requested a *"wash job"*. Mowery said, *"I growled, because it was Christmas Eve and I didn't want to do any car washing"*. But when Smith insisted that only the roof of the car be washed, Mowery agreed. Mowery is the only person to testify that Elmo Smith was ever seen driving. Remember, a condition of Smith's probation was that he was not permitted to drive. I could find no reported testimony of Mowery having identified Smith as driving the stolen BelAir.

Charles Gorman, another witness said that, on the night Maryann disappeared he noticed a man in a car similar to the Brigg's car parked at 9282 Ridge Pike, the home of his girlfriend, with the interior dome light on. In court that location was reported as being *"Near the spot where the body was found"*. In reality it is .08 mile from where the body was found. Cirillo did not ask Gorman if Smith resembled the man. Remarkably, neither did the defense attorneys.

Monday August 29.1960

Jurors went to the Adams County jail to examine the BelAir.

Tuesday August 30, 1960

Elmo Smith was the only person to testify today after his court appointed counsel began their case without an opening address.

During questioning in which the death car route was traced Smith insisted his familiarity with the route when he led Montgomery County authorities over the streets and roads was because Philadelphia police took him there first and pointed out the places where garments, and the

57

body, were thrown from the car. Smith stated that, *"Except for pictures, I had never seen the girl."* In recounting his whereabouts on the evening of December 28, 1959 he left his home because his brother, who he didn't get along with, was coming to visit his mother. He walked to his doctor's office in Norristown with the intention of making an appointment, but, arriving there found the office closed. He then walked to a movie theater in Norristown, decided he did not like the movie and left. Smith then began walking toward his home. He stopped at a drug store and talked with a clerk, but made no purchase. He continued walking toward his home, stopping under a railroad bridge because it was raining very hard. He stopped at a service station to use the restroom getting the key from the attendant. Smith said he recalled stopping at a diner to get a snack, but did not remember if it was as he was walking to Norristown or back from Norristown. He then walked to his home arriving there before midnight, he was certain of the time because a condition of his probation was a midnight curfew. He was certain his mother heard him enter their house.

Smith said that, *"The point in the confession where he and the girl made love in the back seat of the car was suggested by Chief Charles Moody. I don't recall telling the police we had intercourse, it was Chief Moody's idea that I got in the back seat and he suggested intercourse".*

As the cross-examination got started Cirillo waved the seven page confession in front of Smith and asked, *"Does this contain the truth?"* Smith replied, *"No it is not the truth".* Cirillo questioned Smith for 3 1/2 hours. The two men clashed again and again as Smith steadfastly denied killing Maryann. Smith twice told Cirillo, *"I'm not afraid to face you or anyone else".*

Time after time Smith stated that he couldn't remember or couldn't recall incidents in the confession, that he didn't remember making them, or that the statement was wrong.

Under direct examination by Gilbert High, Smith said, *"I was beaten and forced to make the confession"*. He said further, *"I was not given the opportunity to read the confession, and it was not read to me"*. He did sign the document.

Smith said the one reason he signed the confession was that he wanted to go before a jury. He then cast blame for the murder on Thomas Bryson, *"My feelings about Thomas Bryson were not believed by the police. I felt I could come into court and say why I suspect the man"*.

Wednesday August 31, 1960

Today, once again, Elmo Smith was the only witness for the defense. He told assistant district attorney Cirillo, that the confession which he later repudiated was based on information furnished by police and newspapers, radio and television accounts of Maryann's murder. On the evening Maryann disappeared, Smith reiterated that he walked from Bridgeport to Norristown to see his doctor, but found the office was closed so he returned home. He said that on the way home he stopped at a gas station to use the restroom and had gotten the key from the attendant.

Immediately after Smith's testimony, the state called the detectives of the Philadelphia Special Investigations Squad George Gill, Ronald Votto and Emil Mueller to rebut testimony by Smith that he confessed only because he was beaten by police and feared for his life. Each denied Smith's allegations.

Philadelphia Assistant District Attorney F. Emmett Fitzpatrick was also a witness for the prosecution and denied telling Smith, *"I'll keep coming back until you change your story"*.

Joseph Pignolia, 17, a Norristown service station attendant where Smith said he used the restroom, testified that he did not see Smith at the station on the night of the murder.

Paul Frickles, a foreman at the Lukens Steel Plant, Coatesville testified that Thomas Bryson was at the plant on the night of December 28.

The final witness for the prosecution was Dr. Gibbaro Squillace, Philadelphia police surgeon, who stated that on January 5, the day Smith was arrested, he found scratches on Smith. He did not give the location of the scratches on Smith's body, nor did Dr. Squillace testify about the scratches being made by human fingernails. Smith told Squillace he was scratched while moving rosebushes. He said that blood had gotten onto his blue work jacket which he had taken to the dry cleaner and dyed green.

There was little cross examination by the defense and then the defense rested, but only after the stipulation was made that, *"Smith's mother, had she been present, would have testified that her son was in their Bridgeport home about the time Maryann was abducted"*. Mrs. Smith did not attend the trial. Her absence raises questions in itself. Why was she not there at her son's trial, a trial that could, and did, lead to the death of her son? Why, if she was the one person who could offer a solid alibi, was she not there?

Thursday September 1, 1960

Today summations were given by both the prosecution and defense. The verdict was delivered in less than two hours. Guilty. Sarah and Edwin Mitchell were not in the courtroom when the verdict was announced.

When the verdict was first announced, Smith's eyes kept filling up with tears but his face remained expressionless.

Friday September 2, 1960

Today the jury sentenced Smith to death by electrocution. Mrs. Mitchell said, *"I hope God can forgive him"*. Smith declared, *"I am innocent of this case. I never saw her before in my life"*. When Judge Sheely concluded his sentencing with the words, *"May God in his infinite goodness have mercy on your soul"*, Smith bowed his head and replied, *"Your Honor, may God have mercy on all of us"*.

The Execution

Monday April 2, 1962

Joseph R. Daughen, <u>Philadelphia Daily News</u> Staff Writer, reported on the execution of Elmo Smith:

"The first slender shoots of grass were pushing up through the earth and forsythia buds were bursting with the promise of new life as I strode across the prison yard to watch a man die. It was early evening on April 2, 1962, and before the day was over, Elmo Smith, 41, would be a corpse, executed in the name of the citizens of Pennsylvania for the brutal rape-murder of Maryann Mitchell, a pretty, red-haired 16-year-old.

I had covered the investigation and Smith's arrest as a reporter for the *Daily News*. I reported on his trial. Now, as the only Philadelphia reporter present, I would be one of 11 witnesses to see Smith for a final time, in the Death House at Rockview Penitentiary in Bellefonte, a short distance from State College.

The witnesses assembled in the administration building, where Rockview Warden Angelo Cavell was waiting to brief us.

We would be taken to a holding room in the adjacent Death House at 8:50 p.m., 10 minutes before Smith was to die, the warden said. Just before 9 p.m., we would be led into the large, square death chamber on the second floor, where we were to sit silently while Smith's life was snuffed out, Cavell said.

Forget about special last meals, the warden added. There was no such thing. Smith had been served liver and onions, potatoes, lima beans, peach shortcake and coffee, just like the other inmates. He had refused the liver, said the warden.

Cavell said he expected no trouble from Smith because, in his experience, condemned men rarely caused problems. 'The surprising thing is that they all walk in and sit right down", Cavell said. As we walked across the yard toward the Death House, we could see the faces of inmates in other buildings in the minimum-security prison looking down at us. They knew what was happening.

We climbed one flight of curved cement stairs and walked past a row of cells toward an open door. A green tarpaulin shrouded the last cell before the door. Elmo Smith was behind the tarp.

The only sound was the slap of our footsteps as we walked to the gray benches built into the wall and sat down. As if we were one, the group - which included state and local law enforcement officers and reporters - stared mesmerized at the open door. The tension was suffocating.

The electric chair stood on a small platform, straps and wires dangling from it, directly across from us. No screen or glass panel separated us. Cavell stood to our left, holding a telephone connected to Gov. David Lawrence's Indiantown Gap mansion. Between Cavell and the electric chair was an earnest young blond man, a Pittsburgh electrician, who was twisting and turning a series of dials set into a wooden panel on the wall. He was the executioner.

A funereal voice chanting the words to "Nearer My God to Thee" brought a subdued gasp from some of the witnesses. The voice belonged to the Rev. Kenneth Anderson, the Protestant chaplain, who led a shackled Elmo Smith, surrounded by guards, into the room.

Smith's eyes were popping with terror at the enormity awaiting him. His future, his life, would be gone in seconds. Smith walked into the room and, just as Cavell had predicted, sat down in the electric chair. Swiftly, the guards were upon him, lashing his arms and legs to the chair with the straps, fastening electrodes to his ankles and wrists. The popping eyes disappeared behind a dark brown leather mask. The final set of electrodes was placed on Smith's head.

A soft "hummmmmmmmm" filled the room as the executioner turned the dials. Smith shot forward as if he had been catapulted, and my knees instinctively clapped together in anticipation of his landing in my lap. But the straps held him in the chair.

It was 9:02 p.m., and the executioner again turned the dials, triggering another "hummmmmm," but Smith only shuddered this time. Quickly, the electrician sent two more charges coursing through Smith's body, and then he stopped. Dr. J.G. Weizel leaned over and examined Smith. The leather mask had been yanked up onto Smith's forehead when the first shock sent him lunging. His mouth was twisted to the left, and a ribbon of spittle ran down his chin. A faint but unmistakable smell suffused the room, like burnt pork. 'I pronounce Elmo Smith dead,' Dr. Weizel announced, loudly and dramatically, the final punctuation mark in one of the most notorious criminal cases in the area's history. It was 9:04 p.m."

The Theory

Until his death in 1962 Elmo Smith truly believed that Thomas Bryson murdered Maryann. In this theory Bryson may have framed Elmo Smith for the Norristown arson, car theft and eventually the murder of Maryann, but, Thomas Bryson did not murder Maryann. So who did?

Think about it: Maryann Mitchell, while waiting for a bus on Henry Avenue, is holding both an umbrella and a large handbag containing gifts and personal items. She is beaten over the head with a car jack and dragged into a car. When hit, would not the handbag, perhaps some of its contents and the umbrella have fallen to the ground at the Henry Avenue site? There was no evidence found there.

Think further: Maryann's friends Mary Ann Carney and Constance Kearns and the Koller's Diner employees Joseph Salvato and Rose Pulkowski were almost directly across the street from the bus stop. They saw her as she was walking toward the bus stop 112 steps away from them. Not one of them ever testified or accounted seeing a car stop on Henry Avenue or anyone approach Maryann. Not one witness saw Maryann attacked, in an assault, which would have taken considerable time and dramatic motion. The driver, traveling north on Henry Avenue, would have to pull up, get out of the driver's side of the car (which would have faced Koller's Kitchen) with the car jack in hand or walk to the trunk of the car and remove it. He would then hit her over the head with the jack, open the rear door, get her semi-conscious body into the back seat, pick up the umbrella and the handbag, place them into the car, place the bumper jack into the car, go around to the driver's side, get into the car himself and drive away.

No one saw the assault because, in this theory, Maryann got onto the "A" bus, the bus Frank Talbot was driving that evening. It was Frank Talbot who my father believed murdered Maryann Mitchell.

In the Al Richards interview, Clarence Ferguson himself sated that he asked Constance Kearns and Mary Ann Carney where they had last seen Maryann? The girls answered, *"As she crossed Henry Avenue to the bus stop. We saw the bus approaching but we didn't stop to watch Maryann get on"*. In the least, if this is an accurate statement by Constance and Mary Ann, Frank Talbot would have witnessed the assault on Maryann in those few seconds of the girls seeing the bus approaching and the friends not stopping to watch Maryann get on the bus. Maryann either got on the bus or was assaulted at the bus stop in front of Frank Talbot. Frank Talbot was never a suspect! Because Frank Talbot told police that Maryann had never gotten onto the bus, the bus was never forensically tested for evidence.

My father confronted Frank after both men had attended Mass at Holy Family Church on a Sunday following the murder. My father told Frank he suspected him of killing Maryann. From that Sunday on, my father said that, *"Frank stopped receiving communion"*. It is remarkable that my father, Clarence Ferguson and Frank Talbot were all, at one time, members of the same Manayunk Church, Holy Family. Although Ferguson and, eventually Tinneny, would register at Immaculate Heart of Mary Ferguson knew Talbot from Holy Family. Ferguson would never suspect that anyone he knew would be capable of the grotesque murder, let alone a Catholic man who had a family.

The next point for consideration: Recall the lapse of time, which no one could explain, based on the autopsy results, regarding the food contents in Maryann's stomach, especially the pickle.

Frank Talbot had the perfect opportunity to hold Maryann for a period of time. My father suspected that on Monday night Talbot took the Maryann to an abandoned or remote location along his bus route, restrained her, and continued to work until the end of his shift at approximately 2:00 am on Tuesday morning. Later on Tuesday he would be asked by Philadelphia Police if the teenager had gotten onto the bus. He would deny that she had. Tuesday, Frank began his shift and worked until approximately 2:00 am Wednesday. At the end of his shift he picked Maryann up in his personal vehicle. Or perhaps she was held in the trunk of his vehicle. It was then that Talbot brought Maryann the hamburger with the pickle, which she ate. It was then that he raped and savagely murdered the innocent schoolgirl.

This scenario, not the scenario presented in the confession of Elmo Smith, nor the scenario presented by the prosecution, fits the autopsy results Pathologist Marvin Aronson and Montgomery County coroner Dr. John Simpson perfectly, *"death occurred within minutes after the fatal blows and that the body was found ten to twelve hours after death occurred. Maryann died early Wednesday morning close to 2:30 am. There was no possibility she was beaten on Monday evening".*

And then there was the prosecution's contention that Elmo Smith had pulled the body of Maryann from the stolen car and rolled her down into the gully at Barren Hill Road and Harts Lane. According to Elmo Smith's "confession" she was alive. According to the prosecution she was dead. Neither of which really matters because neither was, by any measure, believable based on the forensic evidence.

The body of Maryann was placed carefully in the gully. Her body was posed, on her back, face up. Her arms and legs were outstretched and her underwear was placed over her right arm. It was there, undetected in the darkness of Harts Lane, in that remote gully, that Maryann's body was desecrated; the coke bottle was jammed into her vagina and the tree branch rammed into her rectum. And finally in that unholy spot, the killer would sign his work in red lipstick on the canvas which was her body, "TB" and "101", an arch and radiating lines.

Theories concerning the letters and numbers scrawled on Maryann's abdomen ranged from far-reaching to say the least, to positively absurd at best. And keep in mind Elmo Smith had supposedly given the meaning of the cryptic drawings in his "confession".

There was boundless speculation as to the meaning of the letter and number scrawlings. TB: Thomas Bryson, the initials of Elmo Smith's ex-wife, the numerical letter value 'T' is the 20th letter of the alphabet, 'B' the second letter indication Rt. 202 where the Lafayette Motel was located. "No. 101": The room assigned to Smith at the LaFayette Motel.

In court assistant district attorney Cirillo gave this interpretation as to the meaning of the lipstick drawings on Maryann's body: *"It's the symbol for St. Elmo, the patron Saint of sailors, and a man with a strange name like Elmo would know all about it. The arc and the radial lines constituted Elmo Smith's coat-of-arms".*

While doing research for this book a great deal of time was spent on understanding the public transportation system, routes, and schedules the PTC (Philadelphia Transportation Company) back in 1959. Believing that Frank Talbot had committed the murder, I sought initially to see if he could have had any possible work/stress related motive to kill Maryann since. And indeed there might have been.

In 1959, as a driver on Rt. 61, Talbot's world was in the grips of transition. I cannot venture to guess the effect the transitions had on him, but to say the least, his world was changed dramatically in the years leading up to 1959.

To understand the turmoil, one needs to go back to 1941, the PTC (Philadelphia Transportation Company) converted trolley car Rt.61 to trackless. The 61 was a significant route which connected Center City Philadelphia to Manayunk, diagonally crossing the western part of North Philadelphia on its journey along Ridge Avenue. It intersected 33 trolley car lines and all three transit routes (Market-Frankford El, Broad Street Subway, Ridge Camden Spur), it passed through major industrial areas as well as large residential neighborhoods.

In 1946 select Philadelphia bus routes were transitioning from a track-trolley car system to a trackless-trolley bus system. In that year the Ridge Avenue Trolley Depot, a long-time storage barn for mothballed trolley cars was re-built, and the Rt. 61's base was moved from Allegheny Avenue to the newly renovated Ridge Avenue location. In 1947 the 61 added just over 1/4 mile of run onto Venice Island alongside the Schuylkill River in Manayunk, with a new loop at the end of Flat Rock Road, serving several industries on the island.

In 1955 PTC came under control of NCL (National City Lines) that company owned or controlled more than 100 electric streetcar systems in 45 cities throughout the United States. The company ultimately dismantled these systems and replaced them with bus systems in what became known as the 'Great American streetcar scandal'. With NCL in control, Philadelphia's plans for trackless expansion came to an end. By 1958 the NCL converted the Philadelphia trackless trolley system to a primarily bus system. In 1959, route 61 began being serviced by buses on weekends and holidays. There was an "A" local schedule and an "A" express schedule. In that same year the "A" bus route was extended to Barren Hill Road in Montgomery County, an extension that was not easily accepted by some drivers. In Manayunk and Roxborough one of the trackless trolley buses that were replaced by a bus was trolley bus No. 101...TB 101. Was it a coincidence that Maryann's dead body was found on Barren Hill Road, the "end-of-the-line" for the newly extended "A" bus route back in 1959.

I had an opportunity in June of 2012 to speak with Eleanore "Ellie" Johnston who was 16 years old in 1959 and found Maryann's handbag on the lawn at 9282 Ridge Pike. Charles Gorman, now deceased, was Ellie's brother-in-law. It was Charles who saw the 1958 BelAir 50 feet above the Johnstone home at 9282 Ridge Pike. Ellie recalled her brother-in-law saying that, *"He could see the driver in the car clearly because the dome light was on. It appeared as if the man had pulled over and was looking down and to his right, like he was reading a map. The driver had on a heavy tweed coat and had long dark hair".* According to Ellie, Gorman said, *"He did not see anyone else in the car. The man never got out of the car, nor did Charlie see him throw anything out of the car".*

The physical description of the occupant of the BelAir did not fit Elmo Smith. He did not have long dark hair by any stretch of the imagination; he had light brown hair that was groomed short and a receding hairline. And recall again that neither the prosecution nor the defense, in trial testimony, ever asked Charles Gorman if the man in the car resembled or was Elmo Smith.

Without a doubt, the 9282 Ridge Pike location, the sighting of the BelAir and the finding of the purse there, are intriguing and would appear to be fundamental in connecting the car, and the driver of the car, to the murder of Maryann Mitchell. But the initial reports of the events surrounding 9282 Ridge Pike in regard to the homicide, and what was testified to in court at Elmo Smith's trial differ significantly.

On Thursday morning, December 31, 1959 a man named Andrew Johnstone phoned Philadelphia Police informing them that his daughter Eleanore had found a handbag that might have belonged to murder victim Maryann Mitchell. Philadelphia police went to the Johnstone home. The mud covered handbag was empty except for a comb inside. Captain Ferguson himself brought the purse to the Mitchell home for identification. When asked when she had found the purse Eleanor said about 11:30 on Tuesday morning (December 29, 1959).

Innocently, 16-year-old Eleanor asked, "*I wondered if the purse has anything to do with the car Charlie saw?*" That question led police to Charles Gorman, Jr. who was dating Eleanor's older sister Kathleen. Charlie had mentioned to Mr. and Mrs. Johnstone that he had seen a BelAir parked about 50 feet in front of his car outside of their home when he was leaving a couple of nights prior around 11:30 pm. Gorman told police that the car caught his attention because it was identical to his father's car.

Initially when police asked Gorman what night he saw the car he stated *"Tuesday [December 29, 1959], the night before Eleanor found the handbag"*. Meaning Eleanor found the handbag on Wednesday morning [December 30, 1959]. In court Charles Gorman, Jr. testified that he saw the BelAir on Monday, December 28, 1959 at around 11:30 pm.

The next piece of the theory centers around the location where Maryann's wallet and Peter Gunn shoes were found: According to trial testimony, in brush atop the elevated corner of Ridge Pike and Barren Hill Road.

My father would, throughout his life, recount how he and another police officer had gone to Ridge Pike and Barren Hill Road, on their own time, to do an experiment. They wanted to see if it was possible to throw items similar to Maryann's, from a car, into the location where Elmo Smith had supposedly thrown Maryann's.

According to the prosecution, Smith assaulted Maryann at Henry Avenue and Walnut Lane and drove north on Henry Avenue. He then detoured off of Henry Avenue onto Ridge Avenue with Maryann in the back seat of the car. As he drove he tossed at least one shoe from her handbag onto Ridge Avenue below Domino Lane. He continued driving on Ridge, stopping at 9282 Ridge Pike, and continued to Barren Hill Road turning left. At this point, while making the left turn, Smith allegedly threw the wallet and shoes out the front driver's side window into the brush atop the elevated corner.

My father said that he tried numerous times to throw the items from the driver's side of the car and on no attempt did it come close to the location where Maryann's wallet and shoes were found. He could not reach the top of the elevated corner. Throughout his life my father would say, *"It would only be possible to reach that spot by throwing from a bus or a truck traveling on south on Ridge Pike"*.

EPILOG

The Review headline in the August 26, 1960 edition boldly announced **"4 Detectives to Claim Rewards in Murder Case"**. The accompanying article goes on to state that the four detectives of the Philadelphia Special Investigations Unit, Emil Muller, Allen Hersh, George Gill, and Ronald Votter will claim all of the reward money offered for the apprehension and conviction of the persons responsible for the murder of Maryann Mitchell.

The bulk of the reward money $1,000.00 was offered by D.V. Aspen, president of Aspen-Hill Manufacturing Company located in East Falls, PA. Edwin Mitchell was employed by that firm as a weaver. Mr. Aspen had the following provision in regard to the reward: The decision as to whom the money should go is to be reached by Edgar E. Mitchell, chief of police of Whitemarsh Township: Chief detective Charles G. Moody of Montgomery county and Philadelphia Police Commissioner Thomas Gibbons. Fergie's Boys laid claim to the reward, but did not collect it.

In July of 1961 the $1,000.00 reward money was shared three ways: The Bridgeport Police Department of Montgomery County received $500.00 which was placed into the police pension fund. Charles Gorman who reported seeing the stolen Briggs BelAir a short distance from 9282 Ridge Pike on the night Maryann disappeared received $250.00. Eleanor Johnstone, the sister-in-law of Charles Gorman, who found Maryann's purse on the lawn at 9282 Ridge Pike received the final $250.00.

On March 22, 1967 Philadelphia police laboratory technician Agnes Mallatratt Douglas resigned from that position. She had been employed there since 1958. She listed *"personal reasons"* as her explanation for the resignation.

A month earlier, during the trial of Paul Delahanty, accused of the 1965 slaying of Bernice Convey in the Hotel Philadelphia, Douglas gave expert testimony. Defense lawyers Patrick Walsh and Lois Forer felt that Douglas' forensic testimony on hair and fibers was *"patently incredible"*. The two attorneys' began looking into the background of Douglas who had stated, under oath, that she had a degree from Temple where she had taken courses in forensics, biology, botany, zoology, and criminal law.

Walsh and Forer exposed Douglas and discredited her during the trial Delahanty trial. They discovered that Douglas had never earned a degree or certificate from Temple. She hadn't graduated from Germantown High School as she had claimed. They discovered that she had not even finished junior high school. The lawyers also questioned Douglas' claim that she had received a favorable review from the American Society of Forensic Pathologists. The organization did not exist. Faced with overwhelming evidence of perjury, Douglas admitted under questioning, that she had falsified her job application. Delahanty was acquitted.

Over eight years, Douglas gave expert testimony in dozens of cases, including two that sent men to the electric chair; the two men were George Mount and Elmo Smith.

In January 2011 Louis Mikens-Thomas, the oldest inmate at Graterford Prison, was released. The 82 year old served more than 40 years for the heinous, 1966 murder of a 12-year-old west Philadelphia girl. A crime he consistently insisted he did not commit. He was freed because *"His conviction was based on bad science, or perhaps even fraudulent science,"* reported Fay Flam, staff reporter for <u>The</u> <u>Philadelphia</u> <u>Inquirer</u>, the "science" methods of Agnes Mallatratt Douglas.

The question was raised previously as to why Mrs. Flossie Smith did not testify at her son Elmo's trial? Why, if she was the one person who could offer an alibi, did she not do so? The answer to that question is a theory, reinforced in the LaFleur interview of Mrs. Smith herself.

The theory: Mrs. Flossie Smith caught Elmo in a lie concerning the watch he had given to Janet Bryson. He had stolen it from the BelAir when it was parked at the LaFayette Motel, not found it under the Conshohocken Bridge as he contended he had. Flossie Smith, because of that lie, questioned her son's innocence. In the LaFleur interview Mrs. Smith states, *"I suppose he's [Elmo] involved in it but I just don't understand about the time and how all of this could have happened. He [Elmo] tells me, 'If I gotta die, Mom, I want to be sure that I did those things. If I did them, I want to die, but I just don't remember.'"*

Yes, Elmo Smith's mother questioned her son's innocence deeply: *"Whatever society says should be done with my son, I will uphold, but all I ask is that I know the truth. People say I am cold hearted to turn against my son. But, if he did these terrible things to that dear little girl, what else can I do. My heart is bursting. All I can say is, I'm sorry".*

And when Flossie Smith spoke those words of sorrow, she knew well the mother to whom she expressed her sediments. In a strange twist of fate Flossie Smith and Sarah Mitchell knew one another. The two mothers worked together, side-by-side, for what was reported in <u>The</u> <u>Review</u> as *"many years"*, at the Bayuk Cigar Company located at Ninth Street and Columbia Avenue. Flossie Smith was a cigar maker and Sarah Mitchell was a cigar inspector. Not only did they work together, each day the two women rode to work together on the train. Sarah Mitchell would board the train at 6:20 every morning at Manayunk and Flossie Smith who got on at Norristown would sit with Sarah. It was a ritual for the two mothers.

It has been said that the prayer book found in the Briggs BelAir belonged to Maryann Mitchell and bore her name. If that were the case, my father's entire theory concerning the murder of Maryann would be invalid. Seeking the truth concerning Maryann's murder, I sought to verify if the prayer book was hers. To do so I contacted the forensic unit of Montgomery County Detectives and spoke with Lt. Michael Gilbert. Lieutenant Gilbert informed me from the start that the actual prayer book was not in the Montgomery County Office. He did have access to photographs of the prayer book. The photographs were taken of the contents of the trunk of the Briggs BelAir when the car was found and on January 5, 1960.

I was able to arrange an appointment to view the photographs. They were 8"x10" black and white prints taken by Philadelphia Police crime scene photographer William Jennings. The spare tire was there, the bumper jack, a document signed by Joseph Briggs and the prayer book.

The prayer book was not what I expected it to be. Being a Catholic, I had always envisioned the prayer book as the little personal kind children received in First Holy Communion kits, a small 3"x 5" prayer book. All of us Catholics had one of those. They were beautiful little keepsakes from our first Holy Communion. Or perhaps, with Maryann being a teenager, and having attended a private Catholic High School, the prayer book might have been a thin, handbook collection of prayers carried and used by Catholics in general.

The prayer book in the photographs was a large generic publication, approximately 6" x 9" and was titled <u>My</u> <u>Sunday</u> <u>Missal</u> <u>&</u> <u>Manual</u> <u>Explained</u> <u>by</u> <u>Fr.</u> <u>Stedman.</u> Four of the photographs were very similar, shot from different angles, showing the full contents of the trunk. There was one photograph that focused on the prayer book. There were no photographs showing any interior pages of the prayer book only the exterior cover.

I asked Lieutenant Gilbert if there were any photographs showing Maryann Mitchell's signature. He said, *"There are not"*. I asked him, in his professional opinion as a forensic investigator, if her name was in the book, would the signature have been photographed? Lieutenant Gilbert confirmed, *"Yes, the signature would have been photographed documenting evidence that directly connected the victim to the stolen vehicle"*.

On June 3, 1986, without fanfare, indeed without even saying he had done it, Philadelphia Police Commissioner

Kevin Tucker got rid of the "Inspector's Men" of the Special Investigation Unit.

On November 11, 2010 I went the grave of Maryann at the request of her cousin Al Jarvis. Maryann is buried in Westminster Cemetery, located on Belmont Avenue in the Bala Cynwyd suburb of Philadelphia. I was struck by many things there, and took photographs. Most striking was that the burial site appeared to have been recently disturbed. Secondly, the spelling of Maryann's name on her grave marker differed from all newspaper accounts I had read. On the headstone it is engraved as two separate names "Mary Ann".

Lastly, it was very obvious that someone recently visited the grave. Atop of the headstone lay a single red carnation. A pumpkin and silk flowers, in vibrant autumn colors, were at the rear base of the headstone. On the side of the base there was a glazed ceramic statue of two small children, a boy and a girl being protected by a guardian angel. All of these years later, 16 year-old Maryann Theresa Mitchell continues to be remembered with love.

Since that first visit in November 2010, I have visited the grave of Maryann many times. There are always new gifts of flowers there. On August 23, 2012 while researching the dates of the deaths of Sarah and Edwin Mitchell, Maryann's parents, at the Westminster Cemetery Office I learned why the grave site was disturbed back in 2010. Sarah Mitchell died in 2010 and was buried on November 8, 2010. She lived to be 98 years old and her casket lies atop of that of her beloved only child's casket. In all, there are 25 people buried in the plot. Edwin Mitchell is not buried there although he is buried in Westminster Cemetery. Edwin died in 1973, his burial date June 4, 1973.

I have no doubt that had Maryann's murder occurred in more recent years, my father would have turned to The Pennsylvania Innocence Project on behalf of Elmo Smith. Not for any purpose other than, right is right and wrong is wrong, a man's name is his legacy. Elmo Smith was a son, a brother and a father, a friend, yet, his legacy remains the murder of Maryann Mitchell.

There was no DNA testing back in 1960, if there had been I find myself wondering if things would have turned out differently for Elmo Smith. It is ironic that the first criminal justice application using DNA evidence proved a confessed murderer innocent.

My father's obsession in the search for truth in regard to the murder of Maryann, has become my obsession. In 2004 a movie came out titled "The Five People You Meet In Heaven". When I saw that movie for the first time I remember thinking that: When I die, if I get to go to heaven, I hope Maryann Theresa Mitchell is one of the five people I meet. And if I do get to meet her, you can be certain I will ask her what really happened on December 28th back in 1959.

The memory of Maryann Mitchell is kept alive on the following internet sites:

Blog

www.MarynnMitchell.blogspot.com

FaceBook

Mary Ann Mitchell Homicide/Research & Memories

…please visit, share your thoughts and memories.

IN GOD'S HANDS — Maryann
Mitchell, 16-year-old Manayunk
girl bludgeoned to death by sadistic killer, was buried Monday
after solemn requiem mass at St.
Josaphat's Church. Girl was 11th
grade student at Cecilian Academy,
Mount Airy, and was photographed at retreat early last year.

This is the single, published photograph
of Maryann that appeared in <u>The Review</u>
throughout the year 1960

The Mitchell home (r) at
195 DuPont Street
Photo credit: <u>Actual Detective Stories</u>

The Roxy Theater
6189 Ridge Avenue
Philadelphia, PA 19128
Photo credit: The Review

Joseph Salvato, the manager at Koller's Kitchen
On the night Maryann disappeared
Photo credit: The Review

Crime Scene on Barren Hill Road
Wednesday December 30, 1959
Photo credit: <u>Actual Detective Stories</u>

Sarah and Edwin Mitchell
at the funeral mass for their daughter.
Photo credit: <u>Actual Detective Stories</u>

Captain Clarence J. Ferguson
Head of the Philadelphia Police Special Investigation
Squad
Photo credit: <u>Actual Detective Stories</u>

Elmo Smith
Photo credit: <u>Actual Detective Stories</u>

Joyce Davis
Photo credit: Actual Detective Stories

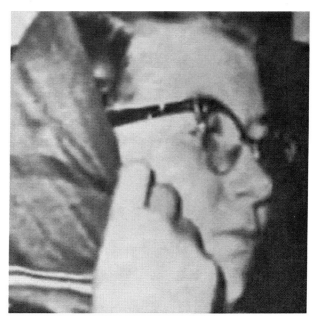

Mrs. Janet Bryson
Photo credit: <u>Actual Detective Stories</u>

TB #101
Serving Manayunk via Ridge Avenue
Photo credit: Volkmer Collection

Crime lab technician Agnes Malatratt Douglas
Photo Credit: File photograph/The Philadelphia Inquirer

The grave stone of Maryann Mitchell
With her name engraved as two separate
names Mary Ann
Westminster Cemetery
2010
Photo credit: Donna Tinneny Persico